THE
BRABANTI BABY

THE
BRABANTI BABY

BY

CATHERINE SPENCER

MILLS & BOON®

*First published in Great Britain 2004
Large Print edition 2004
Harlequin Mills & Boon Limited,
Eton House, 18-24 Paradise Road,
Richmond, Surrey TW9 1SR*

© Spencer Books Limited 2004

ISBN 0 263 18126 X

*Set in Times Roman 16 on 17 pt.
16-1204-58024*

*Printed and bound in Great Britain
by Antony Rowe Ltd, Chippenham, Wiltshire*

CHAPTER ONE

Be CAREFUL and establish your rights from the start, because Gabriel Brabanti is a shark, and given half a chance, he'll eat you alive. There's no middle ground with him, ever. It's his way, or the highway—and I chose the highway!

Her cousin's warning ringing ominously through her mind, Eve took a firmer grip on the infant seat holding her niece, and paused in the entrance to the Gerolama Cassar Executive Arrival Lounge at Luqa, Malta's International Airport.

One among the select group waiting to welcome passengers flying in from Amsterdam was the man himself, Marcia's ex-husband and the father of sweet Nicola Jane, whose birth hadn't ranked high enough on his list of priorities for him to attend it in person. Instead, almost four months after the fact, he'd summoned mother and child to visit him, half a world away from Manhattan.

But had Marcia cooperated? Heavens, no! Marcia only ever did what she wanted, and she wanted *easy, convenient, glamorous.* And the

5

rest, the *untidy* stuff? She palmed that off on to someone else, a fact Eve was so well aware of that she had only herself to blame if she didn't like her present difficult situation.

It had begun innocently enough—and wasn't *that* typical!—with a call from Marcia one evening, when the air-conditioning in Eve's Chicago apartment had failed yet again, her clothes were sticking to her like wet tissue paper, and her resilience sat at an all-time low.

"How *are* you, Evie?" Marcia had cooed effusively. "I *miss* you! It's been too long since we spoke!"

But the preliminaries had soon given way to the real reason for her call. Gabriel Brabanti was flexing his paternal muscles and demanding visitation rights.

"And there's no way I'm putting in a command appearance just because His Highness ordered it," Marcia had spat, her tone changing from sweet to steely, and echoing indignantly over the speakerphone she insisted on using so that Jason, her new husband, could be part of the conversation. "As far as I'm concerned, I never received his letter."

"I don't see how you're going to pull that off," Eve had pointed out. "You just finished saying he had it delivered by courier to the agency, which means you had to sign for it.''

''I don't care! The almighty Signor Brabanti can go to hell! He might be a rich Italian living in Malta and wielding a lot of clout *there,* but he's a nobody in New York.''

Eve heard the rustle of paper, then Jason spoke. ''Might be best to cater to him, butter-cup. From the tone of this letter, he means busi-ness. Either you go to him, which gives you the choice of making the visit short and sweet, or he comes here and hangs around as long as he pleases—and we don't want that, now do we?''

''If you think my showing up with Nicola will put an end to his demands,'' she'd replied, ''you're dreaming, honey. They're just the be-ginning, mark my words.''

A pause, then Jason's voice again. ''What's your take on all this, Eve?''

Wishing she'd let her answering service pick up a message, because becoming embroiled in the permanent crisis which best defined Marcia's life inevitably wound up costing her more than she could afford, Eve said, ''From what you've told me, I have to agree with Jason, Marcia. Either you make the trip to Malta, or Gabriel will come to you. It's your call. Either way, he's obviously determined to see his baby and frankly, he has every right to do so.''

She hadn't needed to be there in person to know that Marcia's mouth had taken on the mulish pout she'd perfected before she turned four. It had announced itself in her petulant reply. ''Then you can be the one to take her to him, because I won't have him hanging around here, and I absolutely will not go back to Malta. And before you turn me down, Eve, let me remind you who came to Chicago to look after your smelly old cat and water your plants, the last time you spent a month lolling around on the Mexican Riviera.''

''For heaven's sake, that was five years ago and Fidelio's been dead nearly two—and he didn't smell, at least no more than you would if you were almost a hundred and forty years old in human years! As for the plants, you managed to kill off every one!''

''Nevertheless, you owe me.''

Eve had been sorely tempted to remind her cousin that, at the time, she'd been desperate to leave New York until the heat died down, after she'd become altogether too friendly with a client whose wife hadn't looked kindly on his wandering eye. But unwilling to shatter Jason's illusions about his brand-new wife, she'd made do with a firm, "I'm well aware that the rare favor you do for someone else invariably comes with a hefty price tag, Marcia. But if you think I'm about to take your baby off your hands and—"

"Why not?" Marcia shot back. "You're forever saying you want to meet her. Well, here's your chance to put your money where your mouth is, and do some serious bonding."

"You're out of your mind!"

Apparently Eve hadn't been the only one who thought so. Even Jason, who had no real stake in any of this, added a shocked protest. "That's going a bit far, buttercup!"

"So's my traipsing off to Malta at a time when your career's at a critical point and you need me around to protect your interests. Who do you think matters more to me, Jason: you or Gabriel?"

"Well," he'd said, "when you put it that way…"

"What other way is there?" Marcia had replied blithely. "Come on, Eve, be a sport! You of all people know how hard it's going to be dragging a baby from one small town to another in the kind of sweltering heat and humidity we get here in the summer."

"Taking a child out of the country involves a bit more than presenting a plane ticket," Eve objected. "There's the small matter of a passport and parental permission. Or are you expecting me to smuggle her aboard in my carry-on bag?"

"I'll make sure you've got all the necessary documentation. You just concentrate on Nicola and make sure *she* knows her mommy loves her."

"And how do I do that, exactly?"

"You'll figure out a way. It's not as if I'm handing her over to some inexperienced stranger, after all. You're a nurse. You deal with babies and children all the time." Marcia had paused for a breath before winding up for her final argument. "Think about it, Eve! You've taken a leave of absence because you're burned out from working twenty-four seven in that flea pit you call a clinic. You need a vacation worse than anyone else I know. And I'm presenting you with the chance for a luxurious holiday on an exotic island in the Mediterranean. Whatever other opinion I hold of my unlamented ex-husband, I'm the first to admit he never settles for anything less than the best, so you'll travel first class all the way, and be waited on hand and foot while you're a guest in his house.

You'd have to be some sort of fool to turn down an offer like that.''

And a bigger fool not to! Yet here she was, complete with sleeping babe, waiting to confront the unpleasant Signor Brabanti whom she'd never met, because Marcia had wasted so little time marrying him that none of her family had known about the wedding until it was over. And before they'd had time to get used to *that* idea, the marriage was over, too.

...Tall, dark and handsome, and so arrogant you won't be able to miss him. Just head for the guy acting as if he owns the place....

So Marcia had described him, but eyeing the group clustered before her now in the executive lounge, Eve saw no one fitting that description. Instead she was approached by a gray-haired man of medium height, in crisp white trousers and a navy blazer with a gold-braided coat of arms emblazoned on the breast pocket. ''Signora Brabanti?'' he inquired.

''Caldwell,'' she said, wondering why he'd think she was her cousin, when she knew Marcia had let Gabriel know she was sending Eve in her place. ''Signorina Caldwell.''

He inclined his head in apology. ''*Scusi.* I am looking for an American with a baby and—''

"You've found her." She gestured at Nicola who, worn-out with screaming pretty much non-stop during the flight from Amsterdam, had at last fallen asleep. "This is Signor Brabanti's daughter."

"*Capisco!* I am Paolo, sent by the *signor* to drive you to the Villa Brabanti."

"He couldn't spare the time to come and meet us himself?"

"The *signor* sends his apologies." Paolo's tone was as neutral as his glance. "A matter of some importance arose which prevented him from being here."

"More important than meeting his daughter?" She raised her eyebrows, making no secret of her disdain. "And here I had the impression he was anxious to see her as soon as possible. Silly me!"

The chauffeur coughed and glanced away, clearly unused to hearing anyone criticize his employer. "You have had a long journey," he murmured soothingly. "If you care to wait in the car, *signorina,* I will collect your luggage, then we will be on our way. You and the *bambina* will soon be home."

Hardly 'home', she thought, following him through the main arrivals hall to the black Mercedes Benz limousine parked directly outside the building. Although it was only a little past seven-thirty in the evening, already it was dark, but floodlights illuminated the handsome curved facade of the airport.

"Allow me, *signorina*." Relieving her of the infant seat, Paolo lifted it into the roomy interior of the car, deftly buckled it in place in the middle of the back seat, and ran a gentle finger down the sleeping baby's cheek. *"Molto bella, si?"*

Although her grasp of Italian was minimal, Eve understood well enough to reply, "Yes, she's beautiful, but I'm afraid all this traveling has been very hard on her."

He murmured sympathetically, and waited for Eve to get settled before handing her the overloaded diaper bag and her purse, then disappeared into the building again to retrieve the rest of her luggage, a task he accomplished with amazing speed and efficiency. Within minutes, he was behind the wheel and the limousine was gliding away from the curb, and dovetailing smoothly into the stream of traffic heading toward Valletta.

"A bit of history goes a very long way with me, but you'll soak up all that antiquity," Marcia had predicted. "You can't turn a corner anywhere in Malta, especially not Valletta, without coming smack up against some ancient relic.''

Although Gabriel lived just outside the city itself, as the car headed northeast and the ramparts of the capital came into floodlit view, Eve could well understand her cousin's remarks. Even after dark and from a distance of several miles, those soaring, massive walls, built centuries before by the Knights of Saint John, made an impressive sight, and despite all her reservations about making the trip, she found herself hoping for a few days to herself, to explore the famous islands.

Any such ambition faded, the minute the limousine swept through the iron gates guarding the entrance to the Villa Brabanti. The house rose up in the night, huge and dark, a barren, looming pile of stone with not so much as a speck of light shining from its windows. Only the moon, cool as ice, glimmered on the glass panes. Not for a second could she imagine leaving Nicola in the care of a man who chose to live in the sort of mansion lifted right out of a gothic horror movie.

''Are you quite sure we're expected?'' she asked Paolo, an undeniable quiver of apprehension slithering down her spine. ''I don't see any sign of the welcome mat being rolled out.''

"It is the emergency of which I spoke," he explained, coming around to open the limousine's rear door. "Unfortunately the main fusebox in the villa has developed a problem which poses a fire hazard. As you know, *signorina,* Malta has adopted the British electrical system, supplying 240 volts. When trouble arises, it is not something to be ignored. We could roast in our beds otherwise."

Her disquiet increasing with his every word, Eve remained firmly seated and said, "What a comforting thought! Perhaps I'd be better off taking the baby and staying in a hotel until the problem is resolved."

"Quite unnecessary," Paolo assured her. "Signor Brabanti has the situation well in hand."

As if he'd uttered some magical incantation, the property suddenly came alive with light. It poured from the windows, flowed from hidden spotlights in the garden, and fell in a bright golden swath from the open front door to illuminate the forecourt where the limousine stood.

"Per favor, signorina." Paolo extended his hand, less in invitation than command. "The *signor* will have heard us arrive." He didn't need to add, *And he doesn't like to be kept waiting.*

The way his tone verged on the imperious said it for him.

"Very well." Suspending her reservations for the present, Eve leaned over to unbuckle Nicola's infant seat. "Come on, munchkin. We might as well get this over with."

The night air lay warm and heavy with the scent of flowers. A cluster of fat white blooms hung ghostlike over the edge of a stone retaining wall sturdy enough to hold back an army. Tall palm trees stood sentinel-like along either side of the long driveway leading to the forecourt. Somewhere to the right, below a sweep of lawn, the soft boom and swish of waves breaking over rocks swept the silence like a lullaby.

"This way, *signorina.*"

Paolo ushered her through the front door and into an entrance hall of such grand proportions that it would have done justice to a royal residence. Checkerboard black and white marble tiles covered the floor. Tapestries, faded by age to softly muted tones of ecru and rose and blue, hung from the walls. Directly in front of her, a magnificent marble staircase rose to a central landing, then branched in two to lead to a gallery that ran around the entire second story. Overhead, some forty feet above the ground floor, frescoed cherubs cavorted among a sea of clouds around the perimeter of a domed ceiling with a stained-glass window at its center.

Gazing around, Eve's first impressions of the place underwent change. Old the house might be, but "elegant" more properly described it than "gothic"; "sumptuous" rather than "barren." In fact, she was so entranced with the visual feast surrounding her that she failed to notice a recessed door at the rear of the hall, until it thudded open and the figure of a man appeared silhouetted on the threshold.

Even without Marcia's description, Eve would have recognized him as Gabriel Brabanti. Never mind that the door cast him in such deep shadow that she couldn't tell whether he was handsome as sin, or homely as a board fence. Only the lord and master of the manor could have exuded such presence; such an air of unshakeable, aristocratic authority.

For a second or two, he remained motionless and fixed her in an unblinking gaze, stroking his thumb the entire time over the barrel of the enormous steel flashlight he carried. The intensity of his stare, not to mention the way he caressed the flashlight as if it were a weapon he was debating using, unnerved Eve enough. But when he finally approached her, crossing the wide expanse of marble floor in long, purposeful strides, it took all her considerable willpower not to cringe against the tapestry-hung wall.

He did not look like a father eager to see his baby for the first time. He looked coldly outraged by the intrusion of strangers in his home.

''Who the devil are you?'' he asked, his voice rich as textured velvet, his accent an intriguing mix of Italian overlaid with Harvard English.

Flabbergasted, Eve stared at him. Up close, he was all lean, hard angles and olive skin burnished by the sun. A tall, elegant creature of exquisite proportions; broad across the shoulders, deep in the chest, narrow at the waist.

And his face? He had the face of an irate angel. A face at once so arresting it stole a person's breath away, and so darkly brooding it chilled the blood.

His eyes, she noticed with a faint sense of shock, were a remarkable shade of crystal clear blue. Against the contrasting fringe of dense black lashes and olive skin, they were astonishingly beautiful. As for his mouth…her own ran dry just thinking about it.

Marcia's description of him as dark and handsome ran pitifully short of the mark. He was the epitome of male beauty; a god among mortals. A sight to make rational men grind their teeth in envy, and sophisticated women to fall at his feet. In short, Gabriel Brabanti was the most strikingly beautiful man Eve had ever seen.

"What sort of question is that?" she croaked. "You know very well who I am. Marcia wrote and told you."

But even as she spoke, she knew her words were meaningless, and she knew why. Because, of course, her cousin had done no such thing. Instead Marcia had behaved just as she always did when faced with a sticky situation: she'd lied, then run for cover. It was a habit of such long-standing that the shame was Eve's for having expected anything else.

"What I know," Gabriel Brabanti replied stonily, "is that unless she has undergone extensive cosmetic surgery, you are not my ex-wife. As for her having written to me, apart from a brief note advising me that she would be arriving today, I've had no contact with Marcia since her equally brief message informing me of my daughter's birth."

Still stunned by his appearance and feeling like an utter fool because of it, Eve said, "She's never been much of a letter writer."

His mouth thinned scornfully and she could hardly blame him. Such a lame excuse deserved nothing but contempt. "She appears to possess few commendable qualities. That, however, does not answer my question. Who are *you?*''

''Her cousin, Eve Caldwell.'' She deposited the infant seat on the floor, fumbled to shift the heavy diaper bag from her right arm to her left and thrust out her hand. Discomfited when he ignored it, she rushed to explain, ''I'm Nicola's aunt. Sort of—well, not really. Technically I suppose she's really my first cousin once removed. But Marcia and I are like sisters—twins, even. Our fathers are brothers, and she and I share the same birthday, you see. So it seemed the natural thing for me to assume the role of aunt to her baby.''

''Do you always babble like this in reply to a simple question, Signorina Caldwell?'' he inquired, his gaze never once wavering. ''Or is it something you resort to only when you're nervous?''

''I'm not nervous,'' she said. But that she had to swallow twice and run the tip of her tongue over lips gone suddenly dry made a mockery of her answer.

''You should be. Within minutes of your arrival, you discover your cousin has betrayed your trust. Only a complete simpleton would assume her store of unpleasant surprises ends there.''

His marriage to Marcia might have been brief, Eve decided glumly, but clearly it had lasted long enough for him to get to know her altogether too well. No wonder she hadn't wanted to confront him again. "I can deal with anything Marcia dishes out."

"And so," he said, "can I. I suggest you remember that, Signorina Caldwell, should you ever feel tempted to aid and abet her in any schemes she might be hatching. I'm sure she's regaled you with tales of how miserable and intolerant a husband she found me, but she hasn't the first idea of how formidable an enemy I can be when I really put my mind to it." He stepped closer and made a move toward the infant seat. "Now, having made my position clear, I would like to meet my daughter."

Acting purely on instinct, Eve beat him to it and hauled Nicola out of reach. "She's sleeping."

"So I see. But since I don't expect her to engage in conversation with me, it hardly signifies. Hand her over, *per favor!*"

"Here?" Eve glanced around the vast hall. Impressive and magnificent though it might be from an architectural viewpoint, as a cosy setting for father and daughter to become acquainted, it left a lot to be desired. "Haven't you prepared a nursery?"

"An entire suite, *signorina,*" he assured, his exasperation tinted with amusement. "And all of it well equipped to serve your every need. Don't look so suspicious. I merely wish to hold my daughter, not feed her to the wolves."

Her glance fell from his face to his hands. They looked capable enough, but, "Have you ever held a baby before? It's not the same as handling a parcel, you know. You have to support her head."

"So I've been told."

"And keep a firm grip. Babies have an inborn fear of being dropped."

"I have no intention of dropping her, nor do I intend to take her from you by force. I am, however, rapidly running out of patience. So for the last time, *signorina,* hand her over."

Reluctantly, she did so. He grasped the handle of the infant seat and raised it level with his chest in one smooth swing. "So," he said quietly, his eyes tracking Nicola's tiny features with somber intensity, "this is the child I fathered. She's small."

Small? She was beautiful! Perfect from the top of her downy head to the tips of her dainty little feet! If *small* was the best he could come up with, he didn't deserve her, and Eve would gladly have informed him of the fact if it weren't that alienating him would serve no useful purpose.

"Most babies are, Signor Brabanti," she said, with as much restraint as she could muster.

"I suppose." Continuing to hold the carrier at chest height as easily as if it weighed no more than a loaf of bread, he made his way slowly across the hall and through a doorway on the left.

Following, Eve found herself in a reception room so exquisitely furnished that she couldn't contain a small gasp of pleasure. She'd visited enough museums to recognize that the gorgeous ceiling and wall moldings, the beautiful faded rugs, the inlaid cabinets, and silk-covered sofas were priceless. But it was the combination of color and texture, as much as the antiques themselves, which lent the room such extraordinary distinction.

"There is a problem, Signorina Caldwell?" Elegant eyebrows raised in question, Gabriel paused before the fireplace. "You're perhaps thinking that this isn't a house where a child could roam freely, and play without fear of breaking something irreplaceable?"

She ran a self-conscious hand down her travel-worn suit. A stain marked the lapel of the jacket, where Nicola had spat up during the flight from Amsterdam, and the full skirt was woefully creased. "Actually I'm thinking that, to be in a room like this, I should be wearing formal evening dress—something in heavy slipper satin with a train, and diamonds and pearls."

"The opportunity will arise in due course," he remarked ambiguously, "but for tonight, what you have on will serve well enough. You will have noticed, I'm sure, that I'm not dressed for a night at the opera, either."

Of course she'd noticed! What woman in her right mind wouldn't have, when confronted by such a splendid male specimen? His blue jeans clung to his long legs and molded themselves to his hips like a jealous lover. His shirt, unbuttoned halfway to his waist, ebbed and flowed over the breadth of his chest, allowing tantalizing glimpses of bronze skin and a smattering of dark hair.

With cavalier disregard, he set the infant seat in the middle of an elaborate gilt occasional table, and it was all Eve could do not to utter a protest. "How do I unfasten these restraints?"

"There's a release button here." She hurried forward, unsnapped the buckles holding the safety belts in place, then lifted Nicola out of the seat before it did irreparable damage to the table's delicate surface, and handed her to her father.

He held her with his elbows pressed to his sides, his forearms extended, his hands too inexperienced to know how to scoop up so tiny a burden, and he too unaware to know she'd feel more secure cuddled up against his chest. Instead he stared down at her, the doubtful look on his face speaking volumes. Picking up on his uncertainty, Nicola stretched and let out an annoyed squawk.

He froze. "*Per carita!* She wriggles like an eel!"

"Hold her upright," Eve suggested. "You'll both feel safer that way."

"Like so?" Tentatively he hoisted Nicola so that she rested solidly against his chest, with her head on his shoulder. As if she sensed she'd come home, she turned and burrowed her face against the smooth, tanned skin of his neck, her mouth seeking.

Unexpectedly moved by the sight of the baby, so pink and delicate, nestled trustingly against the man, so dark and strong, Eve swallowed the lump in her throat and said, "Exactly like that."

He made a face. "Why is she's slobbering on me?"

"Because she's hungry." She nodded to where she'd left the diaper bag in the hall. "I've got a bottle of formula out there. If you'll tell me where the kitchen is, I'll go warm it up, then feed her."

He indicated a velvet rope hanging beside the fireplace. "Ring for my housekeeper. She'll heat the bottle. And I," he said flatly, "will feed my daughter. You've done your part by bringing her to me, *signorina*. I'll take over now."

She hadn't been so summarily dismissed since her student nurse days when she'd accidentally stepped on the hospital chief of staff's toe. "Fine," she said, smarting at his high-handed tone, and yanked the bell pull with rather more force than was warranted. "Then you can change her diaper as well. In case you haven't noticed, she's leaking all over your shirt. In fact, give her a bath while you're at it. She could use one, after spending most of the day either in airports or on a jet."

His horrified expression would have been comical if Eve had been in any mood to laugh. But all she could think of was Marcia's warning.

Establish your rights from the start...because given half a chance, he'll eat you alive...!

"Perhaps," he murmured grudgingly, "I'll allow you take care of her needs this one time, after all."

Allow? Oh, the man had gall to spare! "You'll *allow* me to look after my own niece? How big of you!"

For a second too long, they glared at one another, and in that time a turbulent sense of recognition swarmed through the air; a sense that beneath the surface of resentment and rivalry, something much less antagonistic and much more disturbingly erotic, was struggling to emerge.

Even he felt it. "Forgive me, *signorina,*" he said, almost pushing Nicola at her, then backing out of range of that sudden, strange, high-voltage jolt of electricity. "I didn't intend to come across as quite so overbearing. Please attend to my daughter's needs as you see fit. There'll be time enough in the coming weeks for me to become better acquainted with her."

"As you wish," Eve said, feeling oddly disoriented herself. Just as well a pleasant-faced, motherly woman appeared in the doorway and took charge.

Appearing equally relieved by her arrival, Gabriel said, "This is Beryl, my housekeeper. Beryl, my daughter's mother won't be staying with us, after all. Instead Signorina Caldwell is taking her place."

If the housekeeper was surprised by the change in guest arrangements, she was too well-schooled to let it show. *"Si, signor."*

He glanced again at Nicola who'd begun to howl in earnest. Raising his voice over the din, he asked, "How long do you expect it will take to settle her for the night, Signorina Caldwell?"

"An hour, at least."

Eyeing the large gilt pendulum clock on the wall, he said, "Then we'll sit down to dinner at nine-thirty."

"I'd prefer to have a snack in my room."

"Don't push your luck, *signorina!* I've made enough concessions for one night."

"And I've been traveling for the better part of two days."

For a moment, from the way his mouth tightened, she thought they were in for another confrontation. Then, on a long, controlled exhalation, he said, "Indeed you have. How remiss of me to have overlooked that fact. Beryl, show Signorina Caldwell to the suite you've prepared, will you, and make sure she has everything she needs?''

''Certainly, *signor*. And shall I order a light supper while I'm at it?''

''I'll speak to Fabroni on your behalf.'' He glanced again with some alarm at his daughter. ''It would seem you're going to have your hands full, dealing with…that.''

''All right, then.'' She smiled at Eve. ''Come with me, *signorina,* and let's get the little one looked after.''

He watched her follow Beryl out of the room, his brow knit in thought. That his ex-wife was up to something he had no doubt. Unless there was some pressing reason to do so, no normal mother entrusted a young baby to the care of someone else, on a journey taking her halfway around the world, no matter how impeccably trustworthy and capable that person might be.

The question was, what part did the cousin play in all this? Was she merely a pawn in Marcia's latest scheme, or did her big, innocent gray eyes and softly curved mouth serve to disguise yet another devious mind?

He smiled grimly. The day had yet to dawn that Marcia succeeded in manipulating him, and this time was no exception. One way or another, he'd ferret out her true motives, and if either woman thought they'd use a helpless infant to further their own ends, they were in for a very rude awakening.

CHAPTER TWO

BERYL led the way up the marble staircase and along a wide hall to a set of double doors at the end. "Here we are, *signorina*. You're in the tower suite. It's got one of the best views in the whole house, and is very comfortable. Signor Brabanti's given me a free hand setting up the nursery, and I believe you'll find all the supplies you're likely to need, but it's been a long time since I've shopped for a baby. I'd no idea the things you can buy for them, these days." She flung open the doors and stood back. "After you, love."

Stepping over the threshold, Eve found herself in a sitting room furnished in restful shades of aquamarine and cream. Speechless, she gazed around, Marcia's prediction that Gabriel Brabanti spared no expense in making his guests comfortable coming home to roost with a vengeance. The room was beautifully appointed, and large enough that her entire Chicago apartment could have fit in it, with space to spare.

"This is your private *soggiorno,*" Beryl informed her, misinterpreting her stunned silence. "What you'd call a sitting room."

"So I see." Eve blinked, to make sure her eyes weren't deceiving her.

"A bit taken aback, are you?"

"More than a bit! This is all quite...palatial."

"Why don't I take the baby for a minute, while you have a look around?"

"Yes. All right."

Beryl cradled Nicola in the crook of her arm. "The bedroom's down the hall, through that door over there, with a bathroom between it and the nursery, and a little kitchenette beyond that. Let me know if there's something I've overlooked that you'd like to have."

"I can't imagine you've forgotten a thing." Still bemused, Eve wandered about the sitting room, noting the elaborate wall and ceiling moldings, and richly carved door panels. An eighteenth-century ladies' writing desk and bustle chair stood next to a glass and wrought-iron door opening onto a balcony. Beautifully framed antique prints, flanked by Venetian crystal sconces, hung on the wall between two tall oriel windows.

But there were modern touches, too: a telephone on the desk; a brass floor lamp for reading; fresh flowers in a Lalique vase on the low table before the sofa; a stack of paperback novels on a bookshelf next to the small marble fireplace; a remote control for the television set and stereo system housed in a rosewood cabinet.

The bedroom was no less impressive, a vast area of cool oyster-white walls, the same ornate oriel windows as the living room, a carved armoire that surely belonged in a museum, and a similarly carved bed standing so high from the floor that she'd have to climb on the matching footstool beside it to reach the mattress.

But if the chief ambience conveyed by these two rooms was that of an earlier era, the marble bathroom was pure twenty-first century. A steam shower filled one corner. The deep, jetted tub could have accommodated a pair of sumo wrestlers with ease. Even the toilet and bidet went beyond the merely functional in their sleekly elegant lines. As for the gold faucets, thick, velvety towels and profusion of bath oils, powders and lotions…well, they might not have merited notice from European royalty, but they were all a bit overwhelming for a plain little nurse from Chicago.

''There's a portable baby bath in that corner cupboard. It'll fit right next to the wash basin and make it a bit easier on your back when you're bathing the baby,'' Beryl said, coming to stand in the doorway. ''You'd need arms a mile long to lean over that contraption of a tub. A body could drown in it, it's that deep!''

''You're right.'' Eve laughed and looked at her through the mirror above the long vanity. ''Beryl, may I ask you a personal question?''

''Anything you like, as long as it's not how much I weigh,'' the housekeeper said cheerfully.

''It's just that, although you obviously speak Italian fluently, you don't *sound* Italian.''

''That's because I'm not. I'm originally from Manchester, in England.''

''How did you end up in Malta?''

''My husband brought me here for our twenty-fifth wedding anniversary and we both fell in love with the island. He died not long after, and there was nothing left in England for me after that, so I brought his ashes back to the place that held so many happy memories for us, and made a new life for myself. That was eleven years ago, and I haven't regretted it for a second.''

''It sounds as if your marriage was a true love match.''

''Oh, it was! Nothing like that terrible business with the *signor*'s. That wife of his...well, excuse me for saying so, Miss Caldwell, seeing that she's your cousin and all, but there was no pleasing her.''

''Marcia can be difficult.''

The way Beryl's lips clamped together suggested she could have come up with a more choice description, but she made do with a curt, ''That's one way of putting it, I suppose. The real pity, though, is that there had to be a baby thrown into the mess.'' Her voice softened. ''Not that this little mite isn't lovely, because she is. A real little beauty, in fact—but a bit small for four months, if you ask me. Do you think she's getting enough to eat?''

''It's hard to say. I've known her only a couple of days, myself, and most of that time, we've been on the move, so I don't have much of a handle on her eating schedule yet. Compared to some of the babies I see every day, though, she's the picture of health.''

''And she deserves better than to be caught in a tug-of-war between her parents.''

It was on the tip of Eve's tongue to point out that Gabriel Brabanti's limited interest in Nicola hardly left her in much danger of *that,* but to what end? Beryl's loyalty quite rightly lay with her employer. And much though her cousin tested her patience, Eve's lay with Marcia.

"Well, right now, she deserves to be cleaned up and fed. Do you mind going down to the kitchen to heat her bottle while I give her a quick bath?"

"No need for that, love. There's a bottle warmer and a bar refrigerator in the kitchenette. I didn't want you having to go up and down stairs every time she's hungry. Here, you take her, and I'll get the bath ready, then see to the bottle while you sponge her down. Not that I plan to be interfering every other minute, you understand, but you must be a bit worn out yourself after coming all this way. I imagine you could use some help settling in."

In fact, fatigue had begun to take a ferocious toll. Eve's neck and shoulders ached as if she'd just put in a twenty-four hour shift at the clinic. "You really are a gem, Beryl," she said, grateful not just for the housekeeper's thoughtfulness but also for her approachability. "Thank you so much, for everything."

"My pleasure, Miss Caldwell. By the way, there's a bell next to the fireplace in your sitting room, and another in the nursery. Anything you'd like, night or day, just ring, and someone'll be up to see to it for you."

"Right now, only two things come to mind. First, would you mind bringing me the diaper bag from the sitting room? It'll save me having to go through Nicola's suitcase to find a clean sleeper. And second, won't you please call me Eve?''

''I'm not sure the *signor* would approve,'' Beryl said, filling the plastic infant bath half-full of warm water, and laying out towels next to a basket containing baby lotion, cotton swabs, soap and a sponge, before retrieving the diaper bag. ''His ex-wife was always Signora Brabanti to the staff, even though she was American like you, and not given to being quite as formal as he is.''

''This isn't Signor Brabanti's call. I'm not his wife.''

''No, more's the pity! You've got your head screwed on straight, which is a lot more than could be said of *her*.'' She heaved a sigh and checked her watch. ''Well, I've probably said more than I should, so as soon as I've finished here, I'd best be getting back downstairs. It's nearly nine o'clock now. When would you like to have your meal sent up?''

''Why don't we say ten? Nicola should be down for the night by then, and with any luck I'll even have time for a shower.''

*   *   *

She did, but barely, and had only just finished drying her hair when she heard a knock at the door. Tying the strings holding closed her light robe, she went to answer, expecting to find Beryl or another member of the house staff outside.

Instead Gabriel stood there, a guarded smile on his face, a loaded tray in his hands. She wasn't sure which unnerved her more: that he was there to begin with, or that he was smiling. There was nothing particularly friendly in that smile. If anything, it hinted of danger and sent a burst of goose bumps spattering over her skin.

He, too, had showered, and changed into slim-fitting black trousers and a white silk shirt open at the throat. His thick black hair, still slightly damp, curled at his nape. The polished bronze of his skin made his teeth gleam all the whiter.

…Be careful…he's a shark…!

Oh, yes, a very apt description indeed, Marcia! Eve thought, feeling as if she were being pulled into the blue depths of his eyes and stripped of her soul. *And a hungry shark, to boot!*

Oblivious to his effect on her, he strode into the room and deposited the tray on the coffee table. "I don't know about you, *signorina,*" he announced, whipping off the starched linen cloth covering the food, "but I'm starving. We have *insalata* with freshwater crayfish, warm rolls and butter, ripe figs, grapes, a little cheese, some almond tarts...." " He seized the neck of the bottle poking out of a silver ice bucket. "And a very fine white wine."

Giving herself a mental shake, she followed him and eyed the arrangement of crystal, china and sterling grouped around the platters and bowls of food. "Why are there two of every-thing?"

"*Scusi?*" He made a pathetic attempt at in-nocence.

"Don't pretend you haven't noticed. There are two sets of cutlery, two wine glasses, two—"

He raised his elegant black brows. "You do not drink wine?"

"Yes, I drink wine," she said testily.

"*Buono!* Then we have something in com-mon besides an interest in the welfare of my daughter." He half-filled both glasses with the pale gold liquid and passed one to her. "How is she, by the way? Did you have trouble getting her to sleep?"

"No. She was exhausted." She paused long enough to impale him in an indignant glare. "As am I."

"That doesn't come as any surprise. You've covered many miles in the last couple of days."

"Exactly. So you'll understand, I'm sure, when I tell you I'm not up for receiving a guest."

"I'm not a guest, *signorina*. I'm your host."

She drew in a frustrated breath. "I'm well aware of that. But I'm not dressed—"

He dismissed her objection with a careless flick of his hand. "What you're wearing is of no consequence."

Not to him, perhaps, but the knowledge that the thin cotton fabric of her robe and nightgown were more revealing than she cared for, left her feeling at a decided disadvantage. "Then what is? I presume you're here for more than the pleasure of my company?"

"We must talk."

"*Now?*" She glanced pointedly at the carriage clock on the desk. "Can't it wait until tomorrow? I really am very tired."

"But you did ask to be served a snack, did you not?"

"You know very well that I did." She indicated the lavish spread. "Although I wouldn't rate this a 'snack' exactly."

"Nevertheless, now that it's here, you do plan to eat it?"

"Of course! I'd hardly have put your kitchen staff to the trouble of preparing it, otherwise."

"Then since I also have yet to eat, doesn't it make good sense that we do so together, and learn a little more about one another at the same time?"

He wasn't going to back down. That wasn't his style. Rather, he dealt in silent intimidation cloaked in verbal reason, somehow moving in on a person so thoroughly that he stole the air she breathed. Overwhelming her with his size— a big, strong man, both physically and mentally, and well aware that, on his turf, *his* was the last word.

Eve was a guest in his house by default, an understudy for his daughter's mother. As such, she had few rights. And even if that weren't the case, just then she was too worn down to fight him. "Whatever!" she muttered, parking herself in a corner of the sofa, and attempting to tug her robe down far enough to cover her knees.

But he didn't care that she was behaving less than graciously; he only cared about winning.

"That's better," he said, taking a seat next to her, and touched the rim of his glass lightly against hers, causing the crystal to chime like tiny bells. "Welcome to Malta, Signorina Caldwell. May your visit prove pleasant for everyone involved."

"If bulldozing your way into your guests' private quarters against their wishes is your idea of being a good host, I can't imagine either of us finding it pleasant."

He shrugged his massive shoulders and plunged a serving spoon into the crayfish salad. "Time will tell. May I help you to some of this?"

"No, thank you. I can take care of myself."

"As you wish, *signorina.*"

"There's one other thing I wish," she said irritably. "I wish you'd stop with these annoying *'signorinas'* every other breath. Since I have no intention of spending the next several weeks standing on ceremony, and plan to call you Gabriel, you might as well get used to calling me Eve."

"And if I don't?"

"I'll call you Gabriel regardless—to your face, at least. What I call you behind your back rather depends on how well we do, or don't, get along."

Surprisingly he laughed at that, and the change it brought to his face was quite startling. Warmth invaded his cool blue eyes and left flames of amusement dancing there. His mouth softened in a beguiling curve to reveal his white, perfect teeth. She wouldn't have thought it possible for him to become more beautiful, but he put paid to that supposition in devastating fashion. If his scowl put thunder heads to shame, his laughter outdazzled the sun.

No wonder Marcia had been smitten enough to marry him, even if the magic had been short-lived. Looks aside, he possessed a subtle, seductive charm which, should he choose to exercise it, could wreak irreparable damage on a woman's heart.

Shaken by the realization, and disturbingly aware of how close to her he sat, Eve concentrated on the food, helping herself to a small serving of the crayfish salad and a sliver of cheese.

Eyeing the size of the portions on her plate, he said, ''There's not enough there to keep a sparrow alive. Don't tell me you're one of those women so obsessed with her weight that she counts every calorie she puts in her mouth.''

''I won't, if you'll tell me you're not one of those men who thinks it's his God-given right to dish out unsolicited advice every time he opens *his* mouth!''

Smothering another burst of laughter, he allowed his gaze to tour her face with the refined appreciation of a connoisseur. ''No. But I am a man who admires a woman with spirit,'' he purred, the words caressing her as intimately as a kiss.

If he'd leaned over and touched his mouth to hers, she couldn't have responded more shockingly. Her pulse leaped, her throat constricted until she could barely swallow, and her mouth ran dry. More dismaying still, a piercing quiver of sensation shot from her heart to the pit of her stomach.

To pretend such a response was anything other than purely sexual made no more sense than pretending the sun didn't rise every morning. Furious by her body's betrayal, she said, ''Then why didn't you stay married to my cousin? She's got more spirit than any other ten women combined.''

''I beg to differ. Beneath that very shallow air of mature sophistication she projects so well when it suits her to do so, Marcia is little more than a charming but spoiled, and very manipulative child. Sadly, the spoiled too soon overcomes the charming, and one is left to deal with the child and her machinations.''

That he was as astute as he was handsome didn't come as any great surprise. But it did serve to remind Eve that she'd be a fool to underestimate him. ''It takes two to make or break a marriage, surely?''

''Perhaps,'' he said. ''I certainly don't pretend to be blameless in the failure of mine. I freely admit I grew tired of being cast in the role of guardian to a supposedly grown woman, and utterly bored by her attempts to bamboozle me with her little schemes. I never should have married her in the first place.''

''Why did you?''

''Because even I sometimes give in to moments of madness. Marcia arrived on Valletta's social scene and took it by storm. For a while, I was as captivated as everyone else by her foreign ways. I should have known they'd eventually become obstacles neither of us was able to overcome. How is your salad?''

''Excellent, thank you. What do you mean by her *foreign* ways?''

''Our different tastes made it impossible to find a common ground.''

''Which is your polite way of saying she wasn't refined enough for you.''

"Don't put words in my mouth, *signorina*. I meant nothing of the kind, merely that she could not, or would not, recognize that things are done differently here. Malta is a culturally mixed bag, regarded by many as the place where east meets west. Initially Marcia claimed to be fascinated by this aspect of our society, but she soon tired of it and complained we weren't Americanized enough."

"Perhaps because she was homesick."

"Quite possibly. And if so, it was undoubtedly made worse by the fact that her infatuation for me died as quickly as her infatuation with everything else Maltese." He topped up their wineglasses. "You look somewhat dismayed. Have I offended you?"

"No," Eve had to admit. "That's the trouble. Everything you've said so much fits the Marcia I know that I can't begin to defend her."

"Then since we're of the same mind, tell me something." He inched closer. Close enough that his body heat reached out to embrace her. He'd used a faintly spicy soap or shampoo that made her senses swim. Made her want to reach out her hand and touch his skin, his hair.

"Yes?" To her ears at least, her voice emerged in an embarrassing near-whisper thick with expectation.

"Why are *you* here, instead of her?"

Reality smashed aside her brief fantasy with such a vengeance that the succulent morsel of crayfish Eve had popped into her mouth came dangerously close to popping out again. "I already told you," she said, swallowing hastily. "We're cousins."

"I know what you *told* me, Eve," he replied levelly. "Now I want to know the true reason. What's Marcia really up to?"

"Nothing." She dabbed her mouth with her napkin. "She just doesn't want to see you again, that's all."

"Is it?" he said, the inflection in his tone clearly voicing his disbelief. "I very much doubt that."

"I don't know why! You've as good as admitted *you* can't stand to be around *her* for more than five minutes at a stretch, so why wouldn't the reverse be true? It's a perfectly normal response. Divorced people aren't usually the best of friends."

"Yet if they happen also to be parents, they frequently set aside their differences and put the interests of their children ahead of their own."

"Which is what Marcia was doing when she agreed to have Nicola spend the summer with you." Stifling a yawn, she set aside her unfinished meal and made a move to get up from the couch. "Look, I don't mean to be rude, but I really am exhausted, so—"

"There's just one flaw in that argument," he said, closing his long, tanned fingers around her wrist to prevent her from moving. "Marcia's not one to share the limelight unless there's something in it for her, so why would she designate you to show off her baby, when she'd much rather reap all the attention?"

His touch scalded her. Sent the blood boiling through her veins and bolts of sensation shooting up her arm. "In this case," she said breathlessly, "I think it had more to do with the length of time you expected her to stay here. She's married again, as you know, and—"

"I didn't know."

"Oh, dear!" Eve realized the news had come as a complete and unpleasant shock. "I'm so sorry. I just assumed she'd have told you." She stared at him incredulously. "She really didn't mention it?"

"Not a word."

"I can't imagine why not."

"I can. Now that she's found herself a new husband, she'd like to cut me out of the picture altogether and have my daughter call another man 'Papa.'

His grip tightened painfully. Wincing, Eve said, "You're hurting me, Gabriel. Please let go."

He glanced down, seeming almost surprised to find his fingers still locked around wrist. *"Dio!"* he exclaimed ruefully, releasing her at once. "I didn't realize...forgive me." Then, seeing the mark he'd left behind, he touched her again, stroking the pad of his thumb over the redness. "Your skin is so fine, so translucent," he murmured. "Like mother-of-pearl. I'm a brute to have handled you so carelessly."

"You were caught offguard," she said, knowing she'd have to be the most naive fool in the world to believe he meant anything by his words. But although her brain recognized the logic of such reasoning, her pulse operated on a different wavelength and thundered like a runaway locomotive bent on destruction. Striving to control the resulting havoc to her breathing, she went on, "If I'd known Marcia hadn't told you about Jason, I'd have broken the news more tactfully."

His hand drifted down to unfold her fingers and lay bare her palm. "So Marcia fancies herself in love again, does she?"

"It would appear so."

"And when did this marriage take place?"

"The beginning of last month, I believe."

"You *believe?* You mean to say you weren't invited to the wedding?"

"No. I gather it was a very simple civil ceremony, with just two close friends as witnesses. I live in Chicago, and it was hardly worth my making the trip to New York for something which lasted no more than twenty minutes."

"What's your impression of the new husband?"

"I've never actually met him. He was out of town when I picked up Nicola. The closest we've come is talking on the phone. He seemed nice enough."

"He must be extraordinary, that Marcia would choose to remain at his side, instead of being with her child."

"I don't think it's quite that clear cut. He's on tour with a play he's written, and since she's both his wife *and* his agent, she wanted to be with him."

"Just when I insisted on meeting my daughter? How very convenient!"

"As a matter of fact, it was. It spared Marcia having to take Nicola on the road."

"So that she could devote herself to representing the undiscovered genius she married, without being hampered by the demands of a four-month-old baby, you mean?''

''No, that's not what I mean.'' She snatched her hand away from his encroaching fingers. ''Stop twisting my words. She couldn't be in two places at once and had to make a choice. If anything, you should give her credit for trying a bit harder to make this second marriage work.''

''At the expense of our child?''

''Oh, come on, Gabriel! You make it sound as if she abandoned Nicola to a stranger. I assure you I'm well qualified to look after your daughter, and given the way you're spoiling for a fight, it's just as well I'm here and not Marcia. It'll save you arguing about who's the better parent.''

''You have a point,'' he said, the glimmer of a smile curling his mouth, ''and you certainly seem comfortable handling Nicola.''

''I ought to be. I've dealt with enough babies over the years.''

''Ah! You have children of your own?''

''No. I've never been married.''

''The two don't necessarily go hand in hand these days.''

"They do for me," she informed him flatly. "I'm the old-fashioned kind who believes in two-parent families."

"How refreshing!" His smile would have charmed apples off a tree, but there was a watchfulness in his eyes that made Eve wary. "Do you and Marcia have *anything* in common?"

"Yes," she said. "We both love Nicola and want what's best for her."

"Well, I can hardly take issue with that, can I?" He took her hands and drew her up to stand beside him. Her head barely reached his shoulder. "I'd like to look in on my daughter before I leave. Will you come with me?"

Together, they went through to the nursery. A lamp glowed on the dresser, filling the room with soft light. Nicola lay on her back in the crib, with her little arms spread-eagled and her tiny fists curled.

Bracing his hands on the crib rail, Gabriel watched her, his eyes hooded, his expression unreadable. "Will she sleep through until morning?"

"No. She'll need to be fed again around midnight, and again between two and three."

"Then I should be shot for keeping you up so late." He touched her arm. "Tomorrow, you must rest. I'll spend an hour with her after breakfast, before I leave for my office, and another in the late afternoon when I return home. Otherwise, Beryl will look after her.''

''That's not necessary. I'll be fine. I'm used to shift work.''

They were standing close together, speaking in whispers, the way parents might, and the intimacy of it all shimmered between them like a live thing. ''I suspect,'' he said, his gaze burning into hers, ''that you're also used to picking up the slack for others, regardless of what it might cost you.''

''I do what has to be done, but I'm no saint.''

''Nor am I,'' he said, and the way he looked at her made her stomach turn over. ''Nor am I. You'd do well to remember that.''

CHAPTER THREE

WASHED by moonlight, the villa lay at peace. Even the faint cry of the infant upstairs had at last dwindled into sleepy silence. Only he, plagued by misgivings, paced the length of his ground floor study and watched the night slip toward morning.

A three-quarter full bottle of Jack Daniels, something he'd cultivated a taste for during his years at Harvard, stood on the desk, an empty glass beside it. Not even the bourbon could soothe his uneasiness tonight. After the evening just past, his suspicion that Marcia was up to no good had crystallized into certainty.

Their marriage might have lasted less than a year but in that time he'd come to know her well. She was secretive and sly and selfish; a bold-faced liar unhindered by scruples, and completely dedicated to furthering her own interests. And the cousin, Eve, knew it, even though she played her part well, turning her wide-eyed gaze on him and feigning ignorance of the true state of affairs.

She was lying, too, albeit by omission, but exposing her deception would be easy. Under that spirited front she put on, she was vulnerable—and very, very susceptible. He'd noticed how her pulse had raced, how she'd flushed, when he touched her. When they'd stood close together by the baby's crib, he'd seen the agitated rise and fall of her breasts under her robe, and the way his gaze had held her hypnotized.

Unlike her cousin, Eve Caldwell's experience of men was limited. He wouldn't have to work too hard to uncover her secrets and seduce her into becoming his ally.

The realization should have calmed his restlessness and made sleep possible at last. Instead, it left a burning distaste in his mouth which the bourbon couldn't begin to combat. To have to sink to his ex-wife's contemptible level of subterfuge in order to ensure his daughter's welfare offended his sense of decency.

But, a man had to do what a man had to do, and casualties were inevitable in war. Too bad that, in this instance, Marcia had put her cousin directly in the line of fire, and made her the victim. It wasn't fair. But then, the power struggle resulting from a marriage gone sour never was.

*   *   *

For the next few days, Eve took Nicola to visit Gabriel at the appointed time, and he dutifully went through the routine of holding his daughter on his lap, inquiring about her welfare, and handing her back with patent relief when the hour was up.

Eve really wondered why he even bothered with the little thing, he was so uneasy around her. She'd expected better of him. He was from Italy, a country where the "bambino" reigned supreme. *For heaven's sake, cuddle her close!* she felt like scolding him. *Treat her as if she's your own flesh and blood, instead of a stray you found on your doorstep!*

By the end of the first week, however, she noticed he was growing more comfortable around his infant daughter. Once or twice, she caught a hint of real affection in his eyes, of real pleasure in the smile he bestowed on Nicola.

Apart from those times, Eve rarely saw him. She took breakfast and lunch alone in her suite, and when a business crisis of some kind kept him away from home four evenings in a row, she dined alone, too.

Yet whenever she and Gabriel did happen to be in the same room together, the atmosphere between them crackled with a tension that had nothing to do with hostility. Even though the context of their conversations revolved entirely around Nicola and was entirely appropriate, Eve read a different kind of message when his glance happened to collide with hers. The promise in his blue eyes made her forget to be cautious; his smile made her dizzy.

Sometimes, in passing the baby back and forth, their hands would touch. He made such contact seem meaningless, accidental, non-threatening. But it left her feeling exposed, hungry, breathless. She was filled with a sense of anticipation; of something thrilling about to happen.

All that changed on Tuesday, at the beginning of her second week there. At seven-thirty, Beryl showed up with a pot of coffee and insisted on taking over in the nursery.

"After the time you've had, you'll be needing this," she told Eve, swirling cream into a china mug, and topping it up with the rich, aromatic brew. "I heard the baby crying again around two this morning. She sounded colicky, poor little mite."

"I'm sorry she kept you awake, as well," Eve said. "You must be wishing you'd put me in another part of the house where sound doesn't travel so easily."

"Don't worry about me. You're the one who walked the floor with her half the night. Take your coffee outside and get a breath of fresh air, why don't you?"

Stepping out onto her bedroom balcony, Eve breathed in a sigh of sheer pleasure. Except for the lacy black projection of the oriole windows, the limestone walls of the villa rose up, tinted vanilla by the sun. The garden, lush with tropical flowers and trees, sloped down to a crescent of pale sand beyond which lay the deep blue sweep of the Mediterranean.

High overhead, too high for it to disturb the birdsong from a large aviary of finches built into the face of a rock wall, a silver jet streaked across the clear sky, leaving behind a narrow vapor trail. Closer at hand, in the suite behind her, she could hear Beryl crooning to Nicola.

A moment later, the housekeeper appeared in the doorway, with Nicola swaddled in a towel. "By the way, I forgot to tell you that Signor Brabanti asked me to hold off serving breakfast until nine o'clock, and wants you and Nicola to join him."

Ignoring the little leap of her pulse, Eve said, "He's leaving for the office later than usual, then?"

"He's not going to the office at all. He's taking the day off to be with you."

There was no ignoring her body's reaction to that piece of news. Her heart almost jumped out of her chest. "But can he do that? I thought there were problems at work, and he was needed there."

"He can do whatever he likes, love. He's the boss."

Well, of course he was! The idea that he'd be anyone's underling was laughable—and the prospect of spending the day with him, little short of alarming!

Bad enough that the memory of his face and touch kept her awake at night, every bit as much as Nicola's crying. Eve didn't relish the thought of trying to put on a poised front in public, for hours at a stretch, when the very mention of his name was enough to send her into a state of utter disarray.

What had prompted his sudden interest in spending time with her, she wondered, cradling her coffee mug between both hands and leaning on the balcony railing.

As if allowing him into her thoughts was enough to conjure him up in the flesh, a movement in the cove below caught her eye. Glancing down, she saw him emerging from the shallow waves, the water cascading down his body in sun-splintered streaks. He reminded her of some mythical, magnificent sea god—except such creatures usually camouflaged their nakedness with strategically placed garlands, whereas he wore the briefest pair of swimming trunks ever designed by man.

Blithely unaware of his fascinated audience, he sauntered across the beach to retrieve a towel hidden behind a chunk of rock thrusting up through the sand. Afraid her slightest movement would attract his attention, Eve shrank against the sun-warmed stone wall, helpless to tear her gaze away as he dried off his dripping hair, mopped at his broad chest, and last, swabbed the towel up his legs and between his thighs.

And then, to her utter horror, he suddenly straightened and lifted his gaze directly to the balcony where she stood rooted to the spot, her eyes glued to his body as if she'd never before seen how the male of the species was put together. It was all she could not to squeak with embarrassment.

He, on the other hand, wasn't the least perturbed. As casually as any other man might have buttoned up his shirt, he draped the towel around his hips, tucked the ends in place, then raised a hand in greeting. ''Come down for a swim before the day grows too hot,'' he called out.

As if, for her, it could possibly grow any hotter! Already, she was burning up as if she had a fever! Every part of her, from her face to the soles of her feet, had erupted in a fiery blush. How in the world could she ever look him in the eye again?

With extreme difficulty, as she found out soon enough.

''If you're thinking of bathing before breakfast, better not wait too much longer, love,'' Beryl announced, reappearing with Nicola, now bathed and fed, in her arms.

Eve was tempted to invent a headache—anything to avoid having to confront Gabriel again so soon—except what was the point? She could delay matters all she liked, but since she couldn't avoid him indefinitely, there was nothing to be gained be putting off the inevitable.

And what, after all, did she have to feel so self-conscious about? She wasn't the one who'd strutted around practically naked before *him*. If anyone should be red-faced with embarrassment, he should!

Fine talk, and it bolstered her throughout the time it took her to shower and dress. But when, at last, she stood on the threshold of the breakfast room and found him already seated at the table with his nose buried in the morning paper, her composure seeped away like water in a leaky bathtub.

Stop dithering and get it over with! the down-to-earth self she prided herself on being, scolded. *He's just a man, no different from the hundreds of others you've seen. Keep your wild imagination in check, and think of him as just another patient!*

From behind his newspaper, Gabriel spoke. *"Avanti, prego, signorina!* It's quite safe for you to come in. I don't bite."

Feeling as big a fool as she no doubt looked—though how he could see her through several pages of newsprint, defied explanation—she tottered toward the table. "I've brought the baby," she said, for want of a more scintillating reply. "I expect you're ready for her morning visit."

He folded the paper and, setting it aside, rose to his feet. *"Assolutamente!"* he said, taking the infant seat from her and propping it up on the chair next to his so that Nicola faced him. His thick black lashes swept down, as if to hide the sudden tenderness in his eyes as he regarded his daughter. Then, looking up, he bathed Eve in a smile that could only be described as blatantly invitational. "Mostly, though, I wish to apologize to you."

"Me? Why?" It was as well he came around to draw out a chair for her, because her legs were suddenly weak as water and it was all she could do to remain upright. *No* man had the right to be so distractingly gorgeous.

"Because you are my guest and I've been a most neglectful host. It's time I made up for that."

"You're under no such obligation," she replied hastily. "I'm here only as Nicola's... nanny."

"A servant? I think not!" He rested his hands on her shoulders and gave them a little squeeze before returning to his own seat. "My daughter continues to keep you up at night, I'm told."

"A little, yes. She's still very young, and I'm not sure she tolerates her formula as well as she should."

"Probably because she should be receiving mother's milk." His eyes drifted from Eve's face to the bodice of her sundress and remained there. "Is it not common in America for women to breast-feed their infants?"

"Yes," she replied, defying her nipples to acknowledge his scrutiny. "In fact, it's recommended, and the preferred choice of most mothers.''

''But not Marcia.''

''No.''

''Why not?''

''I really don't know. Perhaps you should ask her.''

''I'd gladly do so, if she'd return my calls. I've tried several times to contact her since you got here.''

''Why?'' she said, not about to admit she'd done the same, with singular lack of success. ''To verify that I am who I say I am?''

''No, my dear *signorina*,'' he said mildly. ''To let her know that you and Nicola arrived safely, and keep her informed of our daughter's doings. It strikes me as something any normal mother would want to know. But although I've left messages with her assistant at the agency, I've yet to hear directly from Marcia herself.''

''Probably because she's away. I already told you, as soon as she'd seen us off at Kennedy airport, she joined her husband on tour.''

''So you did. But that hardly renders her incommunicado with the rest of the world—unless he's touring the polar ice cap.''

''There's also the time difference to take into account. New York's six hours behind Malta.''

"I have enough business interests worldwide to be well aware of international time changes, Eve," he reminded her, offering his finger to Nicola, who immediately grasped it in her tiny fist and favored him with a solemn, large-eyed stare.

"Look at that, will you?" he said. "Even though I'm her father, I'm a complete stranger to her. Yet she clings to me with absolute confidence, certain she is safe with me and wraps me around her little heart without even trying. I cannot imagine being indifferent to where, and how, she is."

Ignoring the clutch of emotion inspired by the sight of Nicola's translucent dimpled knuckles curved so trustingly around his long, tanned finger, Eve said, "If you're suggesting Marcia doesn't care—!"

Beryl chose that moment to come into the room with a bowl of peaches, and a basket of warm sweet rolls to go with the curls of butter and preserves already on the table. A young girl accompanied her, bringing in a fresh pot of coffee.

Glad of the interruption, Eve helped herself to the fruit and hoped he'd drop the subject of Marcia's apparent lack of concern for her baby.

Because how could she defend something she herself found hard to understand?

The moment they were alone again, though, Gabriel picked right up where he'd left off. "If I am suggesting she doesn't care," he said, gently disentangling himself from his daughter's grip, and pouring himself more coffee, "I'll be glad to have you prove me wrong. You told me, your first night here, that you're accustomed to being around children, in which case I respect your opinion. Are you a teacher? Is that how you gained your experience?"

"No. I work as a nurse in an inner city health clinic, and I can tell you that the babies I see would consider themselves fortunate beyond their wildest dreams if they had the kind of home Marcia provides for Nicola."

"Are you saying your patients live in poverty?"

"That, of course—and in some cases, it's extreme. But it's not just the grinding misery of being poor that shows in their eyes, it's the violence and neglect that so often go with it. Many of them have learned before they're two years old that they have no future."

His gaze rested on her face with a compassion in its blue depths that, if she'd allowed it, would seriously have undermined her determination to resist him. "You must find that very distressing."

"It breaks my heart, every day."

"And the fact that Marcia appears to treat my daughter like a toy to be cast aside when something more interesting comes along, doesn't?"

"It's not like that, at all!" she insisted heatedly. "You only have to look at Nicola to see that she's well cared for."

He fixed her in such a reproachful stare that she squirmed. "Signorina Eve, a vintage car might be well-cared for, or a garden, or a public park! But a baby deserves better than that, surely? A baby should be treasured, doted upon, adored."

"What makes you think Nicola isn't?"

"On the surface, nothing, although I admit I'd expected her to look a little more robust for her age, and be a good deal more contented than she often is." He flicked a glance at Nicola who, for once, was quite happy gazing at the slow-circling blades of the ceiling fan, then turned his attention again to Eve. "But I see that I'm making you very uncomfortable with my speculations and opinions. Forgive me. I have no right trying to drag you into the middle of what is, after all, a fight between my ex-wife and me." He pushed the basket of sweet rolls closer. "Try these and some of Beryl's excellent home-made preserves. I swear, if she suspects I've spoiled your appetite, she'll make my life a misery.''

The way you made Marcia's? Eve wondered. Because the luxury evident throughout the villa, the sublime Mediterranean setting, the stunning good looks and simmering sensuality of the man seated opposite her—not to mention the charm he could turn on at will—exactly suited Marcia's exotic tastes. Which could only mean that there had to have been something seriously amiss in the marriage, not only for Marcia to walk away from it in the first place, but for her to so adamantly refuse ever to come back or to face Gabriel again.

''I rather doubt anyone could make you miserable without your consent,'' she said, breaking open a roll and buttering it. ''You strike me as being quite…invincible.''

''Does that mean you're not going to talk me out of taking you sightseeing later on?''

''Would it do me any good to try?''

''Not in the least,'' he said, laughter brimming in his voice. ''It's exactly as you suspect: I'm used to having things my way.''

And therein, perhaps, lay the answer to why the marriage had gone wrong, because Marcia was obstinate as a mule. ''Neither you nor my cousin seems to understand the concept of compromise," she observed. "And I don't mind telling you, just how your hard-nosed attitude will ultimately affect Nicola frightens me."

His fingers brushed against hers and grew still. "Don't be afraid, Eve," he said gently. "We're on the same side in this. We both want what's best for my daughter."

She found herself reacting oddly to his touch, with part of her yearning toward his warmth and strength, and another part shrinking from the subtle danger of him. He could say what he liked, but it was what he didn't say that troubled her the most. He wasn't nearly as guileless as he'd like her to believe, and for reasons based on nothing but instinct, she couldn't shake the feeling that if she didn't keep him at arm's length, she'd end up becoming his victim.

"If that's true," she replied, "then you'll agree it would be best if I stayed home with her today. She's had a very rough week of it since she arrived here, and I'd feel better if I were around to keep an eye on her."

He'd decided on the Lamborghini, believing that her seeing the sights from the comfort and vantage point of a convertible would coax her into forgiving him for having dragged her out against her will, and insisting they leave the baby with Beryl.

He should have known better. Stiff with resentment, she sat poker straight, her hands clenched in her lap, her eyes focused directly ahead, even though the city bastions rose up on her right, impressive enough in their age and magnificent engineering grandeur to stop most tourists dead in their tracks.

Already, she'd seen St. John's Cathedral, the harbor, the Grand Master's Palace and the City Gate Bridge, and responded with much the same stony indifference she showed now. No doubt about it: she was sulking!

Undeterred, he continued his running commentary, but admitted to himself that he was beginning to revise his plan of attack. Slow seduction just might not work with a woman like her. She was too disciplined; too sensible. Sweeping her off her feet, quickly before she had time to talk herself out of it, offered a greater chance of success.

"Valletta's known by a number of other names," he recited, swerving the car to avoid a street vendor escaping the heat by pushing his cartload of fruit into the shade of the city walls. "*Città Umilissima,* a gentleman's city, the Fortress City, to name but a few."

"Really," she said, without a flicker of expression. "How interesting."

Certamente! About as interesting as watching paint dry! Frustrated, he swung a sideways glance at her. Before they'd left the villa, she'd changed from the fetching lemon sundress she'd worn at breakfast into a modest flowered skirt which came midway down her calf, and a white cotton blouse. With her hair secured in a long scarf whose ends fluttered behind her like the tails of a kite, and big round sunglasses covering her eyes, she could, if she'd shown an iota of animation, have passed for another Audrey Hepburn. Instead she better resembled a frozen-faced Greta Garbo.

"The so-called 'modern' version of the city was built by the Knights of St. John," he continued doggedly, dragging his attention back to the road. "The architecture, as you've no doubt noticed, is primarily baroque, although there's ample evidence of a much earlier period. It's said that the islands are one big open-air museum dating back seven thousand years."

"Fascinating," she said, which was an outright lie because she was steadfastly refusing to take in a word he said.

"Si. Molto affascinante!" He grimaced. "Almost as fascinating as the fact that I keep all my other ex-wives chained up in the cellar. Your cousin is the only one to have escaped which, of course, explains her eagerness to have you come here in her stead."

"I see."

"You'll probably be next. I've never been able to resist blond American women."

She swung her head to face him, her attention caught at last. "What did you say?"

"Trovaro bionde Americane irresistibile."

"I don't understand Italian."

"Nor English, it would seem." He reached across and removed her sunglasses, which startled her into looking him in the face. "Look, I know you're ticked off because we didn't bring Nicola along, but what was the point when, as you yourself said, she's suffered enough upheaval lately? She'll be perfectly safe with Beryl."

"Beryl doesn't know her routine."

"Nor do you, if what you've told me is true. You met her for the first time little more than a week ago."

"At least I'm used to babies. But Beryl—"

"Will let us know if a problem arises." He patted her knee lightly. "There's such a thing as telephones, *cara mia,* and unlike Marcia, Beryl knows how to use one.''

If he'd touched her with a cattle prod, she couldn't have reacted more violently. Snapping her knees together, she sent him a scorching glare. "Do you *mind!*"

"*Per carita,* will you loosen up? I'm trying to show you a good time, not seduce you in full view of every Dick, Tom and Harry who happens to be looking our way.''

"It's *Tom, Dick and Harry.* If you're going to use colloquialisms, get them right.''

"*Si, Signorina!* Whatever you say, *signorina!* Either way, your virtue's safe—" he let his gaze drift over her, and deliberately dropped his voice to a husky murmur "—*al meno al momento.*"

At least for the moment, la mia bella!

"What did you say?''

"The menu,'' he improvised, not about to translate, and gave her the benefit of his most ingenuous smile. "How is it you say it in English—what shall we put on our lunch menu?''

She regarded him with all the suspicion of a woman confronting a scorpion. "I don't believe that was it, at all—and I don't trust you.''

"*Che peccato!* I am crushed!" He shrugged and swung the car down an alley so narrow, neighbors on either side could have leaned out of their windows and shaken hands with one another.

"You car's likely to be crushed, too, if we meet another vehicle. Slow down, for heaven's sake!"

"It's a one-way thoroughfare, *cara.* We're perfectly safe." He shifted gears, zoomed through an ancient gateway leading to a shady piazza and parked in the shadow of the bastion walls. "Do you like Sicilian food?"

"I don't know that I've ever tried it."

"Then you're in for a treat." He helped her from the car and, cupping her elbow, led her across the piazza to where four tables were set out under dark green umbrellas. "I've been coming to this *trattoria* for years. It's one of the smallest on the island, and arguably one of the best."

She slid into the chair he held out for her, unwound the scarf from her head, and combed her fingers through her hair. "In that case, I'll let you order for me."

"*Buono!*" He nodded to the waiter approaching their table. "*Ciao, Gismondo! Come sta?*"

"Bene, grazie, Signor Brabanti." He nodded at Eve, including her in his reply. *"E lei?"*

"We're ready for one of your excellent lunches—something special for my guest. This is her first experience with authentic Sicilian food. *Cosa raccomanda lei?"*

"Seppia e linguine, fresca stamani." He joined thumb to forefinger and kissed them exuberantly. *"Di prima qualityà!"*

"He recommends the cuttlefish, caught fresh this morning," Gabriel translated for Eve. "It's served in its own black sauce, with pasta. Think you can handle it?"

"I'll try anything once."

He grinned. She was an uptight pain in the neck much of the time, he wasn't sure he trusted her any more than she trusted him, but he found himself liking her anyway. "Good for you. We'll end up friends yet."

He turned back to the waiter, ordered the cuttlefish, with *caponata* to start, and a carafe of Sicilian Pinot Bianco.

"What's *caponata?"* she wanted to know, the minute the wine was poured and they were alone. "Something to do with the Mafia?"

For a moment, he stared at her speechless, at a complete loss to make the connection between organized crime, and aubergine salad. Finally recovering, he said, "Have you had too much sun?"

"No," she muttered, looking embarrassed and wriggling around in her chair in a way that he found far too distracting, "but you have to admit, it sounds a bit like Capone—you know, Al...Capone...."

"You think the chef here is serving him marinated, as an appetizer?"

"Of course not!" She blushed delicately, something else he found altogether too pleasant a diversion. "Stop making fun of me."

"I should take you seriously?"

"You forget, I come from Chicago. I cut my teeth on stories of the lawless gangsters who overran the city during Prohibition. Now, here I am in a country with strong ties to Sicily, the home of the Mafia, eating at a restaurant specializing in Sicilian food, and about to sample *caponata*..."

Bemused, he inspected the contents of his glass. "*Cara,*" he said, "you have the wildest imagination of any woman I've ever met—and no wonder, if gangland exploits made up your childhood reading material. Remind me to supply you with something more suitable, just in case you decide to entertain my daughter with a bedtime story."

"She's a bit too young for that."

"For which I find myself rather grateful!" He toasted her with his glass. *"Salute!"*

"Cheers."

"The wine meets with your approval?"

"It's perfect," she said, taking a sip. "Very light and refreshing."

"Goes well with gangster antipasti, too."

She made a face. "I'm glad you find me so entertaining."

"Actually," he said, deciding she'd given him the opening he needed to pursue his investigation of her more thoroughly, "I find you utterly intriguing. I'd never have guessed you and Marcia were cousins. You're nothing alike. Do you get along well?"

"Yes," she replied. "But only because we don't spend much time together. A day or two in each other's company is about all we can stand before we start bickering. Give us a week together, and we'd be tearing each other limb from limb."

"Why is that?"

Her glance slid sideways, and she took another slow sip of wine to give herself time to come up with an appropriate answer. "We don't see eye to eye on...life."

"In what way?"

"Well, you were married to her, and you've just spent the morning with me. I'd have thought the differences between us would be pretty apparent."

"On the surface, you're less flamboyant than she is."

"She's prettier, you mean." She shrugged. "It's okay, you can come out and say it. It's something I've known all my life."

Then you've been sadly misinformed, he thought. At first glance, Marcia was more striking, more vivid in every way—until a man became aware of the avarice in her rather beady eyes so artfully disguised with makeup, and realized that the full curve of her lower lip sprang less from sensuality than sullenness. At forty, she'd look exactly like what she really was: an overblown, discontented virago, long past her best.

Eve's features, on the other hand, possessed a refinement which age would never steal. Her delicate jaw and high cheekbones alone redeemed her from plainness. Her eyes, large and long-lashed, reflected a compassionate and gentle spirit. As for her mouth…he looked away, disturbed to discover how very kissable he found her mouth.

Of course, in time he *did* plan to kiss her, but becoming enamored of doing so was not part of his plan. "It has nothing to do with looks," he said, topping up her glass. "She is less inhibited, less cool and distant. You I find to be very...repressed."

Sampling the wine seemed to give her the courage to speak her mind. "That's because I'm very uncomfortable around you," she said, raising her eyes to meet his.

"Why is that?"

Another wave of color washed over her face, deeper than the last. "Never mind."

"Ah," he said, knowing very well why. "You are referring to being caught spying on me from your balcony, this morning."

She lifted her chin and speared him with a lofty glance. "I wasn't spying." She paused just long enough to bury a hiccup. "But I'd appreciate it if, in future, you wouldn't...*flaunt* yourself so blatantly."

"Consider me thoroughly chastised," he said, keeping a straight face with difficulty. "It won't happen again. In future when I feel the need for exercise, I'll swim in the pool."

"You have a pool?"

"Not the kind you're used to. The shoreline on the south side of the property has a natural rock basin which I've modified to accommodate a saltwater pool.''

''Then why don't you use it?''

''Because I enjoy the open sea. I can cover more distance and enjoy the challenge of swimming against the current. But the only place that gives easy access is the beach below your windows.''

''Well, please don't feel you have to give that up because I'm staying here. Just be more... circumspect.''

''I could do that, Eve,'' he said wryly. ''Or you could agree not to look.''

She set her glass down on the table with a thump. ''Since we're obviously not going to agree on the subject, can we please talk about something else?''

''Of course. Let's go back to Marcia and why you don't see eye to eye on life. What, in particular, do you disagree on?''

''Becoming involved with one man while she's carrying another man's baby, for a start!''

''Exactly when did the new husband come on the scene,'' he asked, doing his damnedest not to appear too interested.

''I can't say for sure.'' She wrinkled her brow in thought and pursed her delicious mouth. ''I guess I first heard about him just before Nicola was born. I think the fact that I was so critical of the whole arrangement is one reason she didn't invite me to the wedding, or let me know about the birth until Nicola was nearly a month old.''

''You, too?'' He couldn't quite contain his surprise at that. ''Didn't it strike you as odd that she'd wait so long to let her family know she'd had a baby?''

''Well, you know Marcia,'' she said, dipping into her wine again. ''Once she goes off into one of her sulks, it takes a while for her to come out again.''

''Oh, yes! I lived through enough of those to last me a lifetime. But I wonder if, in this instance, her actions had more to do with resentment that she was pregnant in the first place. It's not easy to make a fresh start with someone new if you're dragging along a lot of old baggage from a previous relationship.'' He leaned back and regarded her thoughtfully. ''How would you describe her attitude to Nicola? Would you call her a devoted mother?''

Eve stared at him, and he thought she looked a little glassy-eyed. A long way from drunk, certainly, since she'd had little more than one glass of wine, but that was just enough to make her less cautious in what she said.

"Well, yes! Very devoted. She even initiated a day-care nursery at the agency so that she can keep Nicola close while she's working."

"Very commendable of her, I'm sure! And how does the new husband deal with all of this?"

"He seems very accepting of the fact that, in marrying her, he took on an instant family." She frowned again. "Although, now that I come to think about it, he wasn't very keen on you going to New York."

"He probably didn't like the idea of his predecessor showing up at the front door."

"Probably not," she said, giving him a frank once-over. "I imagine most men would find you a very tough act to follow."

He laughed. "Did you just give me a compliment, *signorina?*"

"Don't let it go to your head! All I meant is, you're successful, and he's not—at least, not yet. But that doesn't make him any less of a man."

Genuinely curious, Gabriel asked, "What, in your opinion, *does* it take for a man to measure up?"

"Certainly not how much money he makes or how much power he wields," she said without hesitation.

"Then what?"

"His capacity to love. His kindness, his loyalty, his inner strength. His willingness to share all of himself with a woman. Being brave enough and big enough to let her know when he's hurting or afraid."

"Most men find that difficult. It goes against the grain for us to admit to weakness."

"I don't see it as weak. I think it takes enormous courage to acknowledge you're not always in charge, that you can't wrestle every circumstance to suit your ends."

Her answer disturbed him more than he cared to admit. She'd identified aspects of his own character which he couldn't deny. He did hold his emotions in check. Did find it difficult to share his innermost thoughts.

As for admitting to fear...*Dio,* that would be the day! A man remained in control only as long as he presented an invincible front to the world. The instant he showed weakness or doubt, he left himself open to attack from his enemies—and although, in Gabriel's case, they wisely remained hidden, that didn't mean they weren't there. No man who'd achieved his level of prosperity was ever free of the envy of others less fortunate.

And yet, looking at the woman sitting across from him now, he wished it weren't so. He envied her simple, straightforward philosophy. Wished he could share it. He didn't pretend to know her well, but instinct told him she possessed a sincerity and integrity his ex-wife had never known.

Eve Caldwell, he thought on a sudden surge of regret, was the kind of woman he should have married. She'd never have betrayed him the way Marcia had. And he wouldn't now be in the position of playing second-fiddle father to his own child.

CHAPTER FOUR

E<small>VE</small> didn't like the way he sank into sudden silence. Gabriel Brabanti wasn't the kind of man to stare aimlessly into space, content to do nothing but run his forefinger slowly around the rim of his wineglass. Something was brewing behind that handsome, impassive face. The probing questions he'd leveled at her in the last half hour attested to that.

"Grazie," he murmured absently, as Gismondo set a basket of bread and their first course before them.

Caponata, Eve discovered, consisted of eggplant, celery, olives and capers, drizzled in olive oil. Nothing sinister about that. But Gabriel, who'd claimed this was one of his favorite *trattorias,* showed no interest in the food he'd ordered with such care. More evidence that his brain was engaged elsewhere.

"What killed your appetite?" she asked. "Was it something I said? Did I offend you with my comments about men?"

He shook his head, the way a person might if he'd nodded off in the middle of a conversation, and looked at her in faint astonishment, as if he couldn't quite recall who she was. "Not in the least. But you *have* given me food for thought."

No great surprise in that! "Oh, dear!" she breathed in mock concern. "Should I be worried?"

"No. You've helped me gain some perspective, that's all." Although he toyed with his fork, he still didn't eat. Instead, he watched her. "You seem to be enjoying the *caponata.* Did I make a good choice?"

"Mmm-hmm." She mopped at a drop of olive oil threatening to dribble down her chin. "In case you haven't guessed, eating's one of my favorite pastimes."

"I wouldn't have guessed from looking at you. You're not carrying an ounce of extra fat."

"That's because I usually run two miles a day."

He speared a sliver of eggplant. "What else do you like to do?"

"Read, watch movies, cook."

"Do you like to shop?"

She laughed. "Of course I like to shop! I'm a woman, aren't I?"

"Oh, yes," he said, holding her in a gaze so scorching that a shudder of sensation shot the length of her. "You're very much a woman."

The laughter died in her throat. "It was a rhetorical question, Gabriel!"

He shrugged. "So?"

"So I wasn't fishing for compliments."

"It never occurred to me that you were." He turned his attention to his salad again. "We have many interesting shops in Valletta, everything from chic boutiques to street markets. Would you like to explore them?"

"Maybe," she said cautiously, "but not today."

And not with him. The more time they spent together, the greater the pull of that unearthly sexual awareness between them, and the weaker the safety barrier of guarded suspicion they'd once exhibited toward one another. The adversarial glint in his eye was gone, and if it weren't completely ludicrous, she'd have thought he'd forgotten she was Marcia's cousin and, by association, someone not to be trusted.

And all *that* proved was that he'd been right in wondering if she'd had too much sun. Add wine to the mix, and small wonder her judgment was off.

"Not today," he agreed. "But very soon."

"And why is that?"

"Because I imagine you'll want to shop for different clothes."

She glanced around, hoping to catch their waiter's eye. He lounged in the *trattoria* doorway, oblivious to anything but the sunlight streaming through the branches of a lemon tree. "What makes you think those I already have won't suffice?"

"Maybe they will," Gabriel said. "Maybe Marcia warned you what to expect, and you came prepared." His hand, coming down hard on hers and clasping her fingers in an unforgiving grip, jolted her attention back to him. "And maybe," he said, imprisoning her startled gaze in his, "I need to make it clear that, when you are with me, Eve, you do not cast your eyes around at other men."

She snatched her hand away, refusing to acknowledge how, even though his voice washed over her in icy displeasure, his touch burned, filling her with delicious, forbidden heat.

"I am not 'with' you," she retaliated, a spurt of anger temporarily rescuing her from an attraction she neither needed nor understood, "and please understand that I feel in no way obligated to defend myself against your outrageous accusation. But, just for the record, I'm trying to catch our waiter's attention because I'd like a glass of water.''

He smacked the heel of his hand to his forehead. ''*Idiota!* Forgive me, *cara!* I should have known better.'' He turned to Gismondo and raised one sleek, dark eyebrow. It was enough. The waiter almost fell over himself in his eagerness to attend to the almighty Signor Brabanti's bidding.

''You didn't have to go overboard,'' she protested, when she saw that he'd ordered a bottle of sparkling mineral water. ''What comes out of the tap would have been good enough.''

''Not so,'' Gabriel said. ''Nothing cleanses the palate and aids digestion like *San Pellegrino,* bottled right where it gushes free, high in the Italian Alps. And it's the very least I could do to atone for my stupidity.''

''It is refreshing.'' Cradling the chilled water glass in her hand, she regarded him curiously. ''What did you mean, a moment ago, about my being prepared because Marcia had warned me what to expect? Prepared for what?''

''The social life you'll enjoy during your stay in Malta.''

''I'm here to look after Nicola, not make an entrance into society.''

"You're my daughter's blood relation and that makes you family. I will not allow you, or anyone else, to treat you like an employee. If you wish to spend most of your days taking care of Nicola, I won't try to stop you. Heaven knows she can only benefit from such undivided attention. But I insist that you let Beryl or one of the other women on my staff take over for you in the evenings."

"So that I can do what? Paint my toe nails and watch television?"

A halfsmile softened his mouth. "This is a small island and I have many friends and acquaintances, Eve. Word's spread that you are here, and they are anxious to meet this stranger in their midst."

"How's that possible? I arrived only a week ago, and took you completely by surprise."

"Ah, but servants talk—in the morning, when they meet at the bakery or in the fish market to look over the day's catch, or when they pass one another in the park." He lifted one broad shoulder in an amused shrug. "Or, failing all other means, when they have nothing else to do but pick up the phone and report the latest household gossip. And you, *cara mia,* are the flavor of the month, whether or not you like it. Already

I've received several invitations, and even de-clined one on your behalf.''

"Oh?" she said, bristling anew. Not that she cared to find herself the focus of his friends' curiosity, but he had his nerve! "Shouldn't that have been my decision?"

"Possibly. But it was for dinner tonight, and issued at very short notice. You're exhausted, even if you won't admit it, and I didn't want to put you in the awkward position of having to say no to people you've yet to meet. Also, you'd be more comfortable, I believe, if your first in-troduction to society was to take place on fa-miliar territory. For that reason, I've arranged a cocktail party for Friday evening. You'll be more rested by then.''

And less likely to embarrass him by wilting into the lap of one of his "society" friends? "Don't you mean, more presentable—always assuming I manage to find something halfway suitable to wear?"

This time, he slapped the table and appealed to the sky. "I have offended her yet again! How is that possible?"

"Oh, a couple of things come to mind," she said. "Organizing my time without so much as a by-your-leave, for starters. Suggesting my wardrobe belongs in a recycling bin. Taking—"

"I suggested no such thing," he cut in. "From what I've seen, you have excellent fashion sense."

"I don't know how you arrive at that conclusion, considering all you've ever seen me in is the sort of casual thing I'm wearing today."

"I've seen you in other things."

"I wasn't including the suit I arrived in. I'm the first to admit it was a bit the worse for wear."

"I wasn't including it, either." He smiled in unabashed delight. "I was thinking of our supper together, your first evening here, and how charming you looked in your...nighttime ensemble."

To offset the surge of pleasure pricking her skin, she pinched her lips together in a grimace of distaste. "I wish you wouldn't do that."

"Do what?"

"Flirt with me. It's so...meaningless."

"I am Italian," he said, as if that explained and forgave any and all transgressions. "Just as the French enjoy their wines and the Germans their bratwurst, so do Italian men enjoy their women."

"I'd have thought it would be pasta."

"Then you have much to learn, *cara mia.*"

Thankfully, the arrival of their main course put an end to that subject, and for the remainder of the meal they discussed less personal topics. Gabriel explained that Malta had almost no natural water reserves, described the desalination plants built to compensate for this, and his involvement in developing treatment plants for polishing groundwater.

Although he didn't come out and say so, from his comments about his various other enterprises around the globe, Eve gathered he was enormously wealthy. Much more so than even the luxury of his villa suggested.

Yet there was an unassuming other side to him, too; one far removed from the affluent world of high society and international tycoons. ''My grandmother,'' he boasted, over espresso and slices of a rich, sweet cake called cassata, ''made the best meatballs in the world. They were the size of my fist. And her *stromboli…!*'' He rolled his eyes. *''Molto eccellente!''*

''What about your mother? Was she a good cook also?''

He threw back his head and laughed, and Eve, more fascinated by the second, drank in the sight of him, feature by feature. His eyes were bluer than the midday Mediterranean sky, their lashes so dense and soft, they might have been spun from black silk. His teeth gleamed whiter than new-fallen December snow on the shores of Lake Michigan. The lean tanned planes of his face and powerful sweep of his neck were those of an aristocrat.

His shirt, open at the throat, revealed a mist of dark hair and a suggestion of the broad chest beneath the fine, pale gray cotton. As for the rest of him...

She swallowed and looked away. She could describe in minute detail the lean flat plane of his belly, the long muscles in his thighs, the prominent curvature of his masculinity nestled between them, and the way she hadn't been able to tear her enthralled gaze away from any of it. Oh, yes, she knew more than she should about the rest of him.

"Afraid not," he chuckled, and it took her a moment to realize what he was referring to. "My mother came from a well-to-do Roman family where servants catered to her every need. She didn't know one end of a rolling pin from the other, but my father didn't care. He loved her just as she was. It drove my grandmother to distraction! I remember her standing in her kitchen, her hair hanging halfway down her back in a long gray braid, berating my father for being fool enough to marry a woman who wasn't Sicilian and didn't know how to boil water. Those two women had a love-hate relationship until the day my grandmother died.''

''Sounds a little like Marcia and me,'' Eve said. ''We can't live with one another, and can't quite manage to live without.''

''But the difference,'' he said, sobering, ''is that my mother and grandmother had one important thing in common: they both adored my father. With you and Marcia—''

''We have Nicola in common, and we both adore her.''

''I hope you're right,'' he said, but where, a moment before, his eyes had been bright with laughter, they now were full of doubt. ''I'm sure you care deeply for my daughter. But her mother...''

''You really need to give Marcia more credit, Gabriel. I'd hoped everything I've told you would have eased your mind on that score.''

''And I hope your trust in her proves well-founded. God knows, I'll sleep easier at night if I can be sure she won't tire of being a mother, the same way she tired of being a wife.''

Brimming with curiosity, Eve tipped her head to one side and was on the point of asking what he meant by that, when his cell phone rang. A brief exchange followed from which she gathered he was talking to Beryl.

"Better head back," he said a moment later, turning off the phone and signaling for the bill. "Nicola's awake and screaming, and Beryl can't console her."

Just as well, Eve decided, following him to the car and tamping down on the swell of disappointment that their time together had come to an end. Too much undiluted Gabriel Brabanti wasn't good for her. He made her wonder about things she'd be better off ignoring. Crazy things, such as what it might be like to be the woman in his life, when she already knew from her cousin that once he'd captured their hearts, he didn't treat his women well.

He made Eve uneasy, too, with his searching questions and unflattering innuendoes regarding Marcia. It was as if he were building a case against her; collecting evidence that she was unfit to care for Nicola.

Unfit for anything, in fact. The distaste apparent both in his expression and tone of voice when he spoke of her suggested a deep and abiding hostility amounting almost to hate. And from everything her cousin had told her, Eve knew Marcia returned his feelings in full measure.

Why? What had happened to turn a love affair into such bitter estrangement? To smash a marriage beyond repair, even though a child was involved?

Angling herself against the side panel of the convertible's passenger door, Eve studied him covertly behind the concealing lens of her sunglasses, looking for answers. He handled the powerful car with casual flair, weaving expertly in and out of traffic—a man completely in charge of himself and everything around him.

Her gaze fastened on his profile and saw the contradictions imprinted there. The unyielding line of his jaw juxtaposed next to the passionate curve of his mouth; the clear-sighted purpose in his vivid blue eyes softened by the long sensual sweep of his lashes. Lover versus tycoon, with the balance of power shifting from one to the other depending on circumstance.

"Why did you *really* marry Marcia?"

The question burst out of her and she cringed at the bald bluntness of it. His reasons were none of her business. Yet she needed to know. Gabriel Brabanti wasn't a man given to impulse, nor one naive enough to mistake brief infatuation for the depth of commitment that held a marriage together. *So why?*

He took his time answering. "I've often asked myself the same question."

"Did you ever love her?"

"No. But I wanted to. Badly enough to ignore all the reasons why we wouldn't work as a couple."

"Why?" she said again. "It's not as if you couldn't have any woman you wanted. You're...."

Handsome as sin, sexy, charming, sophisticated—and certainly rich, if money's important.

He lifted one eyebrow in amused inquiry. "What am I, Eve?"

"...Eligible enough. So why Marcia?"

"Because she came along at the wrong time. Both my parents had died the previous year, first my mother, from cancer—a horrible, lingering death—then, only weeks later, my father from what his doctors cited as 'indeterminate causes' which, in plain language, boiled down to his having lost the will to live without his beloved Ariana."

"He died of loneliness and a broken heart." Eve nodded her understanding. "I've seen it happen often enough when two people have been together a long time and are especially close. One cannot survive without the other."

"Exactly. And in dealing with my own loss, I realized that though I was more successful than my father, and wealthy beyond even my mother's expectations, I was infinitely poorer than either of them because I'd never known that kind of close connection with another person."

The grief etching his features tore at Eve. She knew the healing power of physical contact and wanted so badly to offer him the silent comfort of a touch. But he wasn't looking for sympathy and he'd resent anything smacking of pity, so she slid her hands under her and sat on them until the urge passed, and said only, "I'm very sorry, Gabriel."

He made a helpless gesture with his hand, a sort of *mea culpa* for a weakness in himself that he despised. "So I went searching for it, instead found Marcia and, as I mentioned once before, was briefly blinded by her dazzle and her zest for life. But what at first seemed exciting very soon became exhausting because she was insatiable. No matter how much I gave, it was never enough."

"Do you think she loved you?"

"She certainly did her best to convince me that she did. But it soon became apparent that what she really loved was the social standing and luxury which came of being married to me. And for that I blame myself. I should have seen through her devoted act sooner, because subtlety was never her strong point. Unfortunately, by the time I came to my senses, we were married—not for better, but most definitely for worse.''

''I don't know that I agree with you—about her marrying solely for money. Her new husband doesn't appear to have two cents to rub together, yet she seems completely besotted with him.''

''I'd like to think that's indeed the case, and that she's chosen the right man this time. But I'm more inclined to believe their wedded bliss has a lot to do with the financial settlement she and I arrived at when we divorced. Add the hefty monthly child support payments I make, and my guess is that the playwright husband isn't too worried about starving in an attic while he waits for success to strike.''

''Dear me,'' Eve said, blowing out a sigh. ''Are you always this cynical?''

He shot her a quick glance. ''Well, you know what she used to have, and you've seen what she has now, so how would you describe her standard of living?''

Lavish. Extravagantly so!

Wishing she'd never started the conversation, Eve said "She has a very nice co-op on the Upper East Side, near Central Park. But I'm sure that's because she wants to provide the best possible home for Nicola."

His mouth twisted in a weary smile. "Are you, Eve? Or are you just hoping that's the case?"

"Does it matter, as long as your daughter ends up the beneficiary?"

"You've put your finger on it exactly: it doesn't matter, *as long as my daughter ends up the beneficiary.* And that, my dear *signorina,* has yet to be established." He swung the convertible through the gates to the villa and swore softly at the sight of another car parked in the forecourt. "Damn! It would seem you're about to make your debut into society today, after all. The De Rafaellis have come calling. Brace yourself, *cara.* You'll find my friend Pierone charming, but his wife Janine is the most avariciously inquisitive woman on the island. She'll question you relentlessly."

"She won't get the chance. I'll be in the nursery, dealing with Nicola, remember?"

"She's probably asleep again by now."

But she wasn't. Beryl met them in the front hall, her normally cheerful face creased with worry, a whimpering Nicola cradled to her ample bosom. "Oh, I'm glad to see you, love," she said, passing the baby to Eve. "There's something not right about this bairn, that she gets so beside herself. She ought to be past that stage by now."

Gabriel came close and stroked his daughter's head. "What do you think, Eve?"

"It's difficult to say." She pressed her hand lightly against Nicola's abdomen. It was rock-hard. "In my experience, most babies have settled into a comfortable routine of eating, smiling, babbling and sleeping by the time they're almost four and a half months old. Most are plump specimens of good health who cry only when they're tired, hungry, or needing to be changed."

"But Nicola doesn't fit that pattern, does she?"

"No. But neither does she exhibit specific signs of illness or abnormality." She propped Nicola on her shoulder, rubbed her cheek against the baby's, and patted her little bottom. "She's not running a fever, she keeps her food down most of the time, and she *is* gaining weight, so I'm not seriously concerned. She's simply an undersized, fussy baby whose diaphragm still isn't strong enough for her to get rid of the gas, and it's causing her a great deal of discomfort.

To prove the point, Nicola chose that moment to let out two monstrous burps, then sank her head sleepily against Eve's neck.

"Well, thank the Lord you've got the magic touch!" Beryl fanned herself with the receiving blanket she'd draped over her arm. "Dear only knows what I'd have done if you hadn't come home when you did."

"She'd have burped for you, instead of me. It just takes her longer than most to get around to doing it, that's all."

"Maybe." Gabriel regarded the baby thoughtfully. "But I want a second medical opinion, just to be on the safe side. Not that I mean to offend you, Eve, but—"

"I'm not in the least offended. It wouldn't hurt to have her checked by a doctor. In fact, I was about to suggest just that."

"Good. Then I'll arrange an appointment with a pediatrician as soon as possible, and we'll go together. In the meantime, since she appears content enough, you'd better both come down and meet our guests."

"They're waiting on the terrace," Beryl informed him dourly. "*She's* trying to worm information out of Leola, that new parlor maid, but I've told the girl to keep her mouth shut unless she wants to find herself out of a job.''

His mouth twitched in the ghost of a smile. ''I can always count on you to keep matters in hand, Beryl,'' he said. ''Come, Eve. Bring the baby and let's get this over with.

Perhaps he should have prepared her, after all. When he introduced Pierone and Janine as the *Conte e Contessa De Rafaelli*, Gabriel saw Eve's eyes widen and knew from the accusing glance she leveled at him that she'd have plenty to say about his omission, later. But he'd thought warning her about Janine had been enough, and that mentioning Pierone's title would merely add unnecessary stress to the meeting.

As it was, Janine wasted no time getting down to business. ''So why you, and not the child's mother?'' she asked, after Gabriel explained Eve's connection to Marcia and her reason for coming to Malta.

''My cousin,'' Eve replied with what he considered to be commendable aplomb, given that Janine was inspecting her as avidly as a boa constrictor about to partake of its first meal in days, ''had other commitments which prevented her from spending the summer here.''

"What sort of commitments?"

"Professional engagements, arranged some time ago, which she felt obliged to honor."

"She didn't waste much time starting back to work, did she?"

Eve shrugged and inclined her head. Unlike Marcia, whose hair owed its sunny glow to expensive salon treatments and showed brown at the roots if she neglected it, Eve was a true blond, although her lashes, Gabriel noticed, were dark as soot with just a hint of gold at the base. "No," she said calmly, lifting her very lovely eyes and pinning Janine in an unapologetic stare. "She wasted no time at all."

"I don't suppose you care, though, not when it means you can spend a month or two here with Gabriel." Janine aimed a sly glance in his direction. "You do know, don't you, my dear, that half the single women in Malta will be out for your blood when word gets around that you've taken up residence at the Villa Brabanti?"

She blushed at that, something Gabriel found utterly endearing. "I'm hardly any sort of threat."

Ah, but she was, more than she could begin to guess! She was different from the women he knew. Different from Marcia. He found her can-

dor refreshing, her lack of pretension engaging.
He guessed she must be in her mid-twenties, yet
there was an innocence about her that made him
wonder if she was still a virgin.

He was disturbed at how much he resented
the thought of another man having introduced
her to intimacy and passion.

"I don't suppose you are," Janine said com-
placently, fixing her in a critical eye. "You're
so... *wholesome*. So thoroughly *down to earth*.
No, I can't see you posing any serious threat to
anyone. What do you do, my dear, when you're
not filling in for your cousin?"

"I'm a nurse."

Janine let out a peal of laughter. "How *de-
lightfully* traditional! I should have known!"

"What do you do?" Eve asked, unperturbed.
"When you're not subjecting total strangers to
the third degree, that is?"

It was Pierone's turn to bellow with laughter
then. "Finally someone with the courage to
match you at your own game, Janine. How do
you like it?"

"I don't," she said, the ice in her voice ri-
valing that in her glass. "I'm insulted, and
frankly astonished, Gabriel, that you're just sitting there and allowing a member of your staff
to address a woman of my rank so rudely."

Flushed with embarrassment, Eve bit her lip and flung him a penitent glance. "I really must apologize, to you, *contessa,* and to you, Gabriel. I don't know what came over me."

He wanted to tell her she had nothing to feel sorry about. That she was like a breath of fresh air, and entirely right to take issue with Janine De Rafaelli's inquisition. Most of all, he wanted to take her face between his hands, and kiss the place where her teeth had sunk into her lip.

"Perhaps I didn't make myself clear when I introduced the two of you," he said, sliding a little closer to her on the settee. "Eve is Marcia's cousin, my daughter's courtesy aunt, a welcome guest in my home, and as far as I'm concerned, *Signora Contessa*, the social equal of anyone here."

"Oh, really?" No question but that Janine was put out by his defending Eve. Her eyes narrowed and her mouth tightened as if drawn together by invisible purse strings. "Well, given that she's related to your ex-wife, we can only pray that she's cut from different cloth. Because another Marcia on the scene is something we can all do without, wouldn't you say, my dear Gabriel?"

CHAPTER FIVE

THERE it was again: a light but persistent tapping, at an hour when everyone should be sound asleep. Balancing Nicola on her shoulder, Eve hurried to the door. "We've disturbed you again. I'm so sorry...!" she whispered, fully expecting to find Beryl outside.

Instead Gabriel stood there and even at two in the morning, with his hair mussed and his eyes at a sleepy half-mast, he managed to look good enough to eat.

"Don't be sorry." Uninvited, he stepped into the suite and closed the door softly. "I heard the baby crying and thought I'd better investigate. I wasn't sure you'd be awake."

"If you couldn't sleep through the noise, I don't know how you thought I'd be able to."

"No need to be so defensive, Eve," he said mildly. "I'm not suggesting you're falling down on the job, just that you might welcome a bit of relief. She's been fussing now for well over an hour."

"I know, and I'm sorry. I didn't mean to snap." She stroked a worried hand up Nicola's back, not nearly as confident in the small hours of Thursday morning as she had been in the middle of the afternoon, two days earlier. "She's been fed, burped and changed, but still she's inconsolable. I'm sorry, Gabriel, but I don't seem to be coping as well as I should. You'd think I'd be able to manage better than this. Heaven knows I've dealt with much worse in my time. But it's different when it's one of your own. Not that Nicola's mine exactly, but I *am* the one responsible for her—"

"You're babbling again, Eve," he chided softly, his gaze so warm, so *kind,* that the hard lump of misery in her chest swelled and threatened to erupt into a flood of tears. "And I now know it means you're running on fatigue and nervous energy, and need a break."

"But I promised Marcia I'd take good care of her baby, and look at me! Worse than useless!" Eve's voice wobbled embarrassingly. "I'm so sorry!"

He pressed his fingers to her mouth. "Stop apologizing! I guarantee Marcia's not losing sleep wondering how this child she claims to love so dearly is faring."

"She would be, if she knew what a mess I'm making of the job." Moving out of range, because having him touch her, even if it was only briefly, left her weak at the knees, Eve leaned wearily against the back of the sofa. "She said Nicola sleeps through the night for her."

"That was probably just part of the sales pitch to persuade you to take over maternal responsibility."

"I don't believe she'd lie about something like this."

"Only because you're too worn out to think straight. Here, give the baby to me before you fall asleep on your feet."

"No. It's *my* job to look after her. I can't ask you to walk the floor with her."

"Why not? Isn't that what parents do when the occasion calls for it?"

Struggling to come to grips with her runaway emotions, she said, "Yes, that's what parents do."

"Then instead of arguing the point, hand her over and go get some rest."

In taking the baby, his hands brushed against Eve's and somehow lingered, but although the contact left her so vibrantly conscious of the feel of his skin on hers that she could hardly breathe, Gabriel appeared totally engrossed in his daughter. He transferred her to the crook of his left arm, his dark head bent attentively as he studied her tiny features. As though sensing she was safe in her father's arms, Nicola gave a hiccupping sigh, and stared at him, the tears strung on her cheeks like minuscule pearls, her eyes wide with wonder.

The moment was sacred; the bonding between parent and child a magical, almost tangible thing. Eve lowered her gaze, knowing she wasn't part of the scene, knowing she should remove herself from it. Yet the powerful, invisible strands linking Gabriel forever to his daughter entrapped her, too, and held her mesmerized.

"You feel it, don't you?"

His question cut through the silence like a bullet. Startled, she looked up and found Gabriel watching her, his eyes scorching her with blue fire. If he'd reached out and touched her intimately, in places reserved for a lover, her response couldn't have been more acute. Warmth swirled through her body, flooding into quiet, innocent corners and bringing them to singing awareness.

"Feel it?" she stammered. "Feel what?"

"The connection between us. The thing I looked for in Marcia and have found, instead, with you."

She wet her lips nervously, afraid of what his words implied. Afraid to admit how readily her heart acknowledged the truth of them. "How's that possible when we've known each other only a few days? The reason we seem so in sync is that we're both focused on your daughter. *She's* the common denominator here, not you and me.''

He shook his head. ''Don't do this, Eve. Don't deny what we both know is really happening. Yes, we're focused on Nicola, but there's something else going on here, something that has to do with man-woman chemistry at work.''

Stress, confusion and just plain tiredness brought the sting of tears to her eyes. ''Stop it, please! I can't deal with this now.''

''So we won't talk about it anymore tonight. But tomorrow...'' He shaped her jaw with his long, strong fingers, his touch full of promise, and tilted her face up to his. ''Tomorrow is, as they say, another day.''

His breath fanned her mouth, a sweet narcotic flavored with a hint of toothpaste. She swayed toward him, felt her eyelids grow heavy, her resistance fade. A tear squeezed free and trickled down her cheek.

He caught it on the back of his finger. ''Ah, making you cry is not what I intended,'' he murmured.

''I know,'' she replied, the words faint as a dying echo. ''And I don't know why I'm being so emotional. I'm not usually like this.''

''You're not usually fighting a losing battle with this, either,'' he said, and looping his free arm around her shoulders, drew her to him and brought his lips down on hers in a kiss so achingly tender that she forgot to breathe. Forgot everything but the miracle of a moment that ended too soon.

''Get some sleep, *la mia bella*,'' he said huskily, putting her from him with marked reluctance. ''You'll see everything much more clearly in the morning. You'll see then that I'm right.''

Right about one thing, certainly: she was exhausted to the point that she could hardly see straight. But *sleep?* He had to be joking! How could she sleep with her mind spinning in circles and her body shimmering from his kiss?

Still, she nodded obediently and backed away, desperate to escape before she said or did something incredibly stupid. Like sink helplessly against him and wrap her arms around his waist, and whisper, *Yes! We* are *connected at some powerful, elemental level. Why else did my heart recognize, the second I met you, that from the moment I was born, every facet of my exis-*

tence was just another step on the long road that finally brought me to your door?

It was beyond absurd! This was real life, not a fairy tale, and no woman with a grain of sense allowed her good judgment to be swayed by a pair of devastating Mediterranean-blue eyes, or a voice as alluring as the dark, exotic alleys crouching between Valletta's ancient buildings. As for the kiss—good grief, she'd been kissed before, with a whole lot more passionate aggression than he'd just shown, and she hadn't let it turn her entire world upside-down. So why such a vehement response this time?

But once she reached her room and despite her mental turmoil, she slept anyway. The second her head hit the pillow, she could feel the world slipping away.

She let it go gladly. Just for a few minutes. Just until she came to her sense….

It took much longer than she expected because when she next became aware, more than four hours had slunk by. Although it was still dark outside, the clock on the night table showed nearly six. And the house was eerily quiet.

Panic struck out of nowhere, conjuring up images too fearful to bear—crib death, suffocation, illness so stealthy and deadly that Nicola had succumbed to it without a murmur.

Breathless with irrational terror, Eve swung her legs over the side of the bed, and raced to the nursery. The crib lay empty, its covers just as she'd left them, but in the rocking chair near the window, Gabriel slept, his elongated shadow etched on the wall beside him by the dim night light.

The shirt he'd thrown on the night before hung unbuttoned over the elastic waist of a pair of cotton jogging pants. His legs sprawled, loose and relaxed. But his hands cupped Nicola's bottom firmly, anchoring her securely as she lay stomach-down on his chest, with her heart beating next to his.

Eve stopped short in the doorway, struck yet again by the contrast of the baby's soft, transparent skin and pale fuzz of hair against the tanned breadth of his chest. She was so small and helpless, so completely adorable.

And he...? In sleep, his mouth curved with a gentleness it seldom allowed itself when he was awake; his face appeared younger and more vulnerable, the arrogance it sometimes wore, subdued. His jaw was stippled with new beard growth, his hair fell over his brow, and his lashes lay like black crescent moons on his cheeks. With every breath, his powerful chest rose and fell in a slow, comforting lullaby of motion for his infant daughter.

Spellbound, Eve captured the picture, her eye photographing every last detail and storing it in her memory, a souvenir to be taken out and looked at, again and again, in the years to come. No matter what other mementoes she acquired during her stay in Malta, this, she knew, would be among her most precious.

At last, with the sky brightening and casting the first pale hint of day through the window, she stole to the kitchenette to prepare a bottle of formula and plug in the coffeemaker. When she returned to the nursery with the bottle, the scene remained exactly as she'd left it.

''Gabriel,'' she whispered, touching him lightly on the shoulder.

He came to with a start, his blue eyes dark and unfocused as his gaze roamed the still-shadowed room before locking onto hers. At once, that same stunning, vibrant electricity charged the atmosphere and try though she might, she couldn't tear her herself free of it. Instead she stood paralyzed, the slow, ponderous beat of her heart measuring the seconds.

Finally he spoke, his voice rough as dark brown sugar. "*Buon giorno, cara. Che ore sono*—what time is it?"

"Just after six."

"So late?" He stretched and rotated his shoulders, careful not to disturb Nicola. "No wonder my back aches. Is that coffee I smell?"

"Yes."

"So...?" His smile was sleepy—and distractingly appealing. "Are you going to offer me a cup, or just stand there in that very fetching nightgown, and force me to beg?"

Curbing the urge to shrink from his gaze, she said, "I was about to change Nicola and give her her morning bottle."

"Let me, instead."

"Even the diaper part?" She eyed him doubtfully. "I seem to recall that's one aspect of fatherhood you weren't too keen to experience."

"But I might as well get used to it, *si?*" He eased himself out of the rocking chair and went to the change table. "Pour us each a coffee, *cara mia,* and don't look so apprehensive. You'll hear me calling for help if I run into trouble."

She tilted one shoulder in agreement. Leaving him to it gave her the chance to find her robe and make herself look more presentable. "Whatever you say. You're the boss."

"There is no boss in this situation, Eve," he replied, an undercurrent of reproof in his tone. "We are equals, with a vested interest in Nicola, and with far more else at stake than either of us first supposed. Hurry back. We have much to talk about."

When she returned, he'd managed the diaper and persuaded Nicola to take half the contents of her bottle. *"Grazie,"* he murmured, accepting the mug of coffee she placed at his elbow, but his attention was centered on the baby. "Tell me, Eve: in your professional opinion, is my daughter quite normal?"

"Normal?" she echoed, perching on the rocking chair footstool with her coffee. "Normal in what way?"

"Not only does she cry a great deal, she appears unnaturally weak to me. When I hold her like this—" he set down the bottle and supported Nicola in a sitting position on his lap so that he could coax a burp out of her "—look how her head bobs around, as if it's in imminent danger of falling off."

Eve smothered a laugh. "That'll stop as her neck grows stronger."

"So the books say. They also say that, by now, it should have happened."

"You've been reading baby books?"

"Indeed yes. Why does that surprise you?"

"Well, you weren't exactly...enthusiastic about the idea of becoming a father, at least not in the beginning."

"And by what right do you arrive at that conclusion?"

She realized at once that, for all his talk of their being equals, of there being a *connection* between them, in criticizing him, she'd overstepped the mark. His tone alone created a chill in the air, and never mind that his expression closed and his eyes narrowed with annoyance.

But it was too late to retract her remark, and nor was she sorry. His initial lack of interest in Nicola nagged at Eve and was one reason she tried so hard to fight her attraction to him. She didn't want to fall in love with a man who allowed business to come between him and his child.

"For a start," she said, trading him cool stare for cool stare, "look how long it took you to get around to asking to see her. Most men would have insisted on being present at her birth."

"Most men would have been informed when the birth was imminent. I was not told until after it had occurred."

"That's not what Marcia told me."

"Then Marcia lied. Again. In light of our acrimonious parting, I can understand that she might not want me at her side during the actual delivery, but I made it very clear that I would be on the first flight to New York the minute she went into labor. But she chose not to let me know until considerably after the fact. Nicola was a week old before I knew she'd arrived."

"If you'd really cared, you'd have gone to New York anyway, well before Marcia's due date."

"And done what? Stayed in a hotel, waiting for the phone to ring? I suspect it wouldn't have changed the outcome one iota. I'd probably still have been the last to learn I had a daughter."

"Not quite," Eve said. "If I remember correctly, Nicola was nearly two weeks old before I heard the news."

"So Marcia didn't want either of us around for the most important event in her life. I wonder why not?"

"From everything I was led to understand, she was on bedrest for the last two months of her pregnancy and faced a difficult delivery. Her doctor recommended that, for the baby's sake, she not expose herself to unnecessary stress.'' Eve shot him an apologetic glance. ''I'm afraid having you around would have made that impossible, Gabriel. By your own admission, things had arrived at a very unpleasant pass between you and her.''

''Without question! But I'm no ogre, Eve. If I'd known there were complications with the pregnancy, I'd have declared a truce.''

''Perhaps, given your history together, she didn't think that was possible.''

''You might be right.'' He cast a troubled glance at Nicola. ''I confess, I'm worried by what you've told me, Eve. Could it be that these difficulties you mention have affected my daughter's development?''

''She didn't suffer brain damage during delivery, if that's what you're thinking. The hospital staff would have checked for any sign of that right away.''

''I'm more concerned that Marcia might done something in the early stages of the pregnancy that wouldn't be so immediately apparent—decided she didn't want the baby, perhaps, and tried to get rid of it. I'm wondering if that's why she waited so long to tell me we were expecting a child. She was in her second trimester before she shared the news with me.''

''Marcia would never have tried to abort her baby,''

She spoke with as much conviction as she could drum up, but Gabriel's doubts started alarm bells ringing in Eve's mind. She really didn't believe Marcia would wilfully destroy a life, but she was a party animal, with a taste for alcohol and, by her own admission, occasionally indulged in what she called ''recreational'' drugs. *Could* she have inadvertently inflicted damage on her unborn baby, perhaps in the early weeks before she realized she was pregnant?

Did that explain why Nicola was so irritable, and undersized for her age? According to her mother, she'd clocked in at a respectable six pounds, twelve ounces but it was Eve's guess that she wasn't much more than ten pounds now. Healthy babies usually doubled their birth weight by three months, yet at over four, Nicola was barely halfway there. Could she, God forbid, be suffering from Fetal Alcohol Syndrome, or the less damaging but equally devastating Fetal Alcohol Effects?

If so, and Marcia knew it, that would explain her adamant refusal to come to Malta or allow Gabriel to visit her in New York. Because although hell might have no fury like a woman scorned, it wouldn't begin to compare with Gabriel's lust for vengeance if he learned his ex-wife was responsible for irreversible damage to his only child.

"I can almost hear the wheels turning in your mind, Eve. What has you looking so solemn?"

"I'm thinking it's just as well you decided to have a doctor take a look at Nicola," she said. "It's the only way to put your mind at rest."

"I have an appointment this morning with a child specialist. Will you come with us?"

"If you like."

"Oh, I like," he said. "I like very much the idea of you at my side. I'm looking forward to showing you off tomorrow night, and in the weeks to come."

"I don't know why. I'm not glamorous and vivacious like Marcia."

"You seem to forget that Marcia turned out not to be the right woman for me."

"I'm not the right woman, either! Gabriel, we're adults, not teenagers. We know better than to think…to let ourselves believe…"

"What—that we have no future together? If that's so, why are you trying so hard to convince yourself? Why not just laugh in my face, in-stead?"

She bit her lip and looked away, unable to deal either with his forthright gaze, or the uncompromising certainty she heard in his voice.

"You see? You cannot, because you know that I speak from my heart, and that yours hears what it says." When she still didn't reply, he resumed feeding Nicola and said, "I'm very glad Marcia sent you in her stead, Eve. You're the one who should be this child's mother. Do you ever think about getting married and starting a family?"

"Occasionally. I think every woman does, at one time or another."

"Is there someone special in your life? Someone you could see filling the role of husband and father to your children?"

She thought of Will Powers, the doctor she worked with at the clinic. They'd started dating about a year ago and settled into a comfortable, companionable relationship with sometimes-sex, no expectations, no pressure—and no spark.

Good thing neither of us is looking for a serious commitment, Eve. Don't know about you, but after thirty-six hours straight at the clinic, I'm too drained to get into anything heavy.

Absolutely.

Want to rent a movie tonight, and send out for pizza?

Sure. I'm too tired to cook.
Your place or mine?
It doesn't matter....

It didn't matter. But it should. "No, there's no one special."

"There is now," Gabriel said. "Now, there's me."

"Well? What's your verdict, Dr. Bianchi?" Gabriel sat forward in the chair, coiled with tension.

Eve knew how he felt. Her breath had been in her throat throughout the specialist's lengthy examination. Carmelo Bianchi had come highly recommended by a friend of Gabriel's who'd worked as a pediatric resident under the doctor. Bianchi's research in infant development had resulted in a wing of a children's hospital in Rome being named after him. He was the best Malta had to offer.

Pocketing his stethoscope, he handed Nicola to Eve. "We'll talk in the other room while the *signorina* dresses the *bambina.*"

"We'll talk here," Gabriel advised him. "Whatever you have to tell me can be said in front of my lady."

My lady? Oh, he had a way with words that reduced a woman to putty in his hands!

"*Va bene.*" The doctor propped one hip on the edge of the examining table, chucked Nicola under the chin, and was rewarded with a wet, gummy smile. "Of course, until we receive the results of the blood tests, I can't give you the complete reassurance you looking for, *signor,* but I can tell you with reasonable certainty that your daughter shows no sign of serious abnormalities. Yes, she's small for more than four months, and not as strong as many other babies her age, but this isn't necessarily significant. No two children grow at the same speed. Some are walking at ten months, others aren't ready until they're well past a year. Some are sitting at six months, others not before eight or even nine."

"What about her crying, the interrupted sleep at night?"

Bianchi laughed. "She is an infant, Signor Brabanti! She hasn't learned to tell the time and doesn't yet know that the night is supposed to be for sleeping. If she's hungry or uncomfortable, she'll cry, regardless of the hour. I can prescribe something to help her through this stage, if you like, but again, there are no fixed rules for how soon such phases might last. I know of perfectly healthy, normal two-year-olds who still don't sleep through the night." Gabriel looked so appalled that the doctor burst out laughing again and added, "If it's of any comfort to you, I know of few who don't outgrow the habit eventually."

"That's some consolation, I suppose!" Gabriel inhaled deeply, and blew out a long breath of relief. "Thank you for seeing us on such short notice, Doctor. I'm sorry if we've wasted your time."

"Don't misunderstand me," Bianchi interrupted. "I'm not seriously concerned about your daughter, but I'm not entirely happy with her, either. If you hadn't told me, I'd never have guessed she was nearly four and a half months old, which leads me to wonder if what she's being fed disagrees with her, possibly because she's been switched too suddenly from mother's milk, or possibly because the mother wasn't able to supply her with enough milk in the first place. Hungry babies don't gain weight as they should, and they cry much more than their well-fed counterparts."

Gabriel threw a glance at Eve. "We don't know that she was ever on mother's milk to begin with."

The doctor's expression betrayed nothing, and all he said was, "A pity. If the supply is there, it's unquestionably the best thing for the child." He reached for his prescription pad and scribbled on it. "I recommend this brand of formula. It's expensive, but—"

"That's not a consideration. Whatever my daughter needs, I'm able to provide."

"*Bene*. Then try this for a week, then bring her back again and we'll see how her weight's doing. And this—" he tore off another sheet and scribbled again "—is the prescription I mentioned. Give her the drops as directed and let me know how she responds."

"We will." Gabriel stood up, and offered his hand. "Thank you again, Doctor."

"There's one more thing. You say there were complications during the latter stages of pregnancy and at delivery."

Again, Gabriel glanced at Eve. "That's our understanding, yes?"

She nodded, aware that the doctor watched the exchange with some interest before turning his attention to Nicola again. "And she is staying with you for the summer?" he inquired, offering her his finger to clutch. "Possibly as long as two months?"

"That's correct," Gabriel said.

"Then I'd like to have copies of her medical records sent over, just to be sure I've not overlooked anything of significance."

"I'll see to it immediately."

Afterward, as they drove away from the clinic, Gabriel said wryly, "Can you believe it? Nicola didn't cry once, the whole time we were in there, and look at her now, sleeping like..."

"A baby?" Eve supplied.

He reached across and caught her hand. "Made me look like something of a fool, didn't she?"

"Not a bit," she said, pure pleasure tingling the length of her arm. "You looked exactly like what you are—a concerned father—and there's nothing wrong with that."

"What about Bianchi? What did you think of him?"

"I found him to be very thorough and think he's absolutely right to want to take a look at Nicola's medical records. You can be sure he'll follow up on anything he suspects might be out of the ordinary. My only question is, do you think Marcia will agree to send them to him?"

"She'd better," Gabriel said grimly. "I've about had it with her cat-and-mouse games. She might as well have dropped off the face of the earth, for all I've heard from her." He squeezed Eve's hand. "But enough about her. My friends are very much looking forward to meeting you at tomorrow night's party. I hope you feel the same way."

"Yes," she said. But it was a lie. If his other friends were anything like Janine De Rafaelli, she'd just as soon never meet any of them!

Raising her fingers, he kissed them. "Don't worry, they're not!"

"Not what?"

"All like Janine."

"How'd you know what I was thinking?"

"It's that connection between us, *cara*," he said smugly. "It tells me everything there is to know about you, and the more I learn, the more I like."

CHAPTER SIX

EARLY on Friday evening, Beryl showed up to
lend a hand getting Nicola ready for her debut
into society.

"You'll find the *signor*'s friends a mixed
bunch, everything from displaced royalty to
government bigwigs," the housekeeper told
Eve, running a soft-bristled baby brush over
Nicola's thatch of hair in an effort to get it to
lie flat. "Most are nice enough, but there'll be
a few who'll treat you as if you're last week's
fish left out too long in the sun. Ignore them is
the best advice I can give you. As long as
you've got him on your side, he's all you need."

Eve smoothed a nervous hand down the dress.
A sleeveless chiffon shift, patterned from neck
to hem in delicate blue and mauve roses over a
plain blue underslip, it had struck her as the ultimate in elegant simplicity when she'd bought
it in Chicago for the gala opening of an art gallery. But would it measure up to Maltese high
society? "If they're anything like the woman I
met on Tuesday…"

"The Contessa De Rafaelli, you mean?" Beryl gave a disparaging snort. "Don't let the title fool you. That one's nothing but a jumped-up nobody—a butcher's daughter from Sheffield who didn't know which fork to use until she married the Count. She doesn't fool the people who matter—those in the know can always tell the difference between crass and class."

"Yet Gabriel considers her a friend."

"Let's just say he puts up with her because he and her husband have been friends since they were boys, and she's now part of the package. Common, that's what she is, under all that fancy dressing. Don't let her put the run on you, love. If she tried for the next ten years, she'd never amount to a tenth the woman you are."

"And the others?"

Beryl slipped dainty white kid shoes on Nicola's feet and fastened the silver buckles. "Well, you'll be given a thorough once-over, no doubt about it. The *signor*'s very eligible— a real catch—and you living under his roof is bound to create a bit of a stir. But it's like I said: stand your ground, and don't let them intimidate you. You're every bit as good as any one of them."

Beryl meant to be comforting, she knew but, more apprehensive by the minute, Eve glowered at herself in the full-length mirror. If her dress hit a hopelessly inadequate note for such a gathering, she had no one but herself to blame. Gabriel had warned her she might need to shop for clothes, but instead of heeding advice she now realized had been offered in good faith, she'd taken offense.

"I won't fit in," she wailed despairingly. "I'm don't even look right!"

Beryl glanced up from putting the finishing touches to Nicola's appearance and swept a critical eye over Eve from the top of her head to the tips of her high-heeled sandals. "You'll do well enough for tonight," she said bluntly, "but I daresay you'll have to shop for a couple of fancier gowns before many more days go by. You'll be attending a few posh 'do's' while you're here, and it'd be remiss of me not to make sure you're properly prepared. Here, the baby's ready at last and judging by the number of cars rolling into the forecourt, the party's already underway. Better not keep folks waiting any longer, love."

At least Marcia had seen to it that her daughter's wardrobe was up to scratch.
Nicola looked adorable in a dress of palest pink ruffled silk, lacy tights, and frilled panties over her diaper. Not only that, she was gurgling hap-

pily. No question but that Dr. Bianchi's medication was working like a charm.

Eve could have used a mild tranquilizer herself. Descending the branched staircase as far as the first landing, knowing several dozen curious pairs of eyes watched her every step, was even more of an ordeal than she'd anticipated. Conversations dribbled to a halt, the clink of crystal and shuffle of feet grew silent.

Bemused, she scanned the well-dressed crowd below, the women exotic as butterflies among the more soberly clad men. She caught the shimmer and sheen of fine silk, the glitter and flash of precious gems, the subdued glimmer of gold. And was dismally conscious that her only adornments were plain pearl studs in her ears and a faux diamond bangle on her wrist.

Her step faltered. If Gabriel hadn't been waiting at the foot of the stairs, she really believed she'd have turned tail and bolted back to her suite with Nicola, whose expectations were easy to meet because all she wanted was to be fed when she hungry, and cuddled when she was upset.

But Gabriel trapped her in his gaze and wouldn't let go. She saw his imperceptible nod of approval, the warmth in his eyes, his smile. They bolstered her courage; made her proud.

Lifting her chin, she smiled back.

In a pale gray suit, with a silver-gray tie and white shirt, he looked wonderful. *Wonderful!* And the way he was looking at *her,* they might have been the only two people left in the world.

Suddenly it was just as Beryl had predicted: never mind the others; *his* opinion was all that mattered.

She continued the rest of the way, his unwavering blue eyes her lodestar. When she'd almost reached the bottom, he came up to meet her, took her free hand and brushed his mouth over her knuckles. *"Cara mia,"* he said, in a voice low enough that only she heard, "you look *squisita! Deliziosa!"*

A quiet joy, unlike anything she'd ever known before, seeped through her and she recognized in that moment that, if he asked, she'd walk through fire for this man. Never mind that they'd met less than two weeks ago. Time was irrelevant, a shifting, ephemeral thing that spanned centuries in a single blink of the universe. She'd known him forever, been waiting for him all her life.

"Grazie," she murmured.

He dropped her a slow wink and took Nicola. She lay cushioned in the crook of his arm, her dress spilling over his sleeve in a froth of ribbon and lace, and let out a chortle of recognition. He closed his other hand over Eve's elbow and ushered her down the last few stairs to where his guests waited and watched.

"My friends," he announced, pride evident in his voice and smile, "may I present my lovely daughter, Nicola, and her equally lovely aunt, *la* Signorina Eve Caldwell."

He said more—something along the lines of his being indebted to her for bringing his daughter to him, and his hope that she'd feel at home under his roof and that his friends would become hers—but what left the most lasting impression on Eve was the faint hum of speculation that arose when, in the course of his introduction, his free arm slipped possessively around her waist.

He meant well, she knew. But although part of her basked in his public display of affection, another part cringed. The fires of gossip had started the day she arrived in Malta, and with every word, every touch, he was stoking the flames higher.

Nor was he done yet. When Thaddo, his houseman, circulated through the crowd with a tray of champagne flutes, Gabriel took two, pressed one into her hand, and raised his glass. "Welcome to Malta, *la mia bella!*"

Again, all eyes fastened on her as the guests echoed his sentiment. Then, as Gabriel was swallowed up by friends wanting to admire his daughter, Eve noticed Janine De Rafaelli whispering in the ear of the woman standing next to her. Nothing pleasant being said there, Eve was sure! Fortunately Pierone sent her an encouraging smile that took some of the sting out of his wife's undeclared antipathy.

Still, Eve didn't know how she'd have fared had a handsome, older woman not come forward and, clasping her warmly by the hand, drawn her into the crowd so that she was no longer standing on isolated display.

"I'm Carolyn Santoro," she said, "and I think I know how you're feeling about now. I came here as an English bride thirty-four years ago and thought I'd never fit into such a tight-knit ex-pat community. As you probably guessed, just about everyone here is of English or Italian descent, and we tend to be cliquish, which doesn't say much for us, does it?"

"I suppose it's true anywhere," Eve replied, so grateful for the woman's kindness that she could have kissed her. "People of similar backgrounds stick together and outsiders have to prove themselves before they become accepted. It's the nature of the beast."

Carolyn laughed. ''Sensible woman! Come and meet my husband, Nico. Because of his work, we've both spent a lot of time in the United States and we love it there. You're from Chicago, aren't you? Wonderful city! I adore shopping at Marshall Field's.''

Nico Santoro was as charming as his wife, and as the conversation grew more animated among the three of them, other people gradually joined their group.

''It's wonderful what you've done for Gabriel by bringing his daughter here and taking such excellent care of her,'' one woman remarked. ''My maid told me the baby's not yet sleeping through the night and you're often up with her for hours. She's lucky to have such a devoted aunt.''

''More than that, Gabriel doesn't look haunted anymore,'' Carolyn added. ''It was very hard on him, knowing he had a child he'd never met. Now that you're here, he's more like his old self again.''

The Contessa De Rafaelli, who'd hovered on the fringe of the group, chose that moment to interpose her vinegary spin on the situation. ''Which hopefully means he's also free to associate with his own kind again. The ex-wife was a huge mistake and one we dearly hope he won't repeat. He should have known better than to think an American would fit in here.''

An embarrassed silence fell which, to Eve's sensitized ears, seemed to last an eternity before a frenzied hum of conversation resumed. Her mouth tight with displeasure, Carolyn drew Eve out to the broad terrace where a long, linen-covered table held an array of hot and cold hors d'oeuvres, and more champagne chilling in silver ice buckets. ''Pay no attention to what you just heard, my dear,'' she instructed sternly. ''Janine is perennially discontented with her lot in life and can't abide seeing someone else happy. Which Gabriel clearly is—for the first time in far too long.''

Perhaps, but even though she eventually met a number of other guests, whose names she promptly forgot but who received her pleasantly enough, it did nothing to lessen Eve's sense of being something of an anomaly in their exclusive circle. Not that they made their feelings known openly, of course. They were too well-bred to stare or comment, but she felt their veiled curiosity burning into her back like an open flame.

Finally one woman came right out and asked the question they'd probably all been wondering about. ''Not that it isn't a pleasure to meet you,

Eve, but what on earth would persuade a mother to be separated from her new baby for even a day, let alone a month or more?''

Eve hesitated. She'd invoked Janine's wrath by stonewalling her when she'd asked the same question, and gotten away with it because Gabriel had been there to run interference. She was on her own now, though, and from the way the *contessa* was practically salivating, Eve knew she wouldn't be so lucky a second time.

Trapped in an almost tangible web of curiosity, she searched for an answer that wouldn't add to the gossip already at fever point. Explaining that Marcia had a new husband, was busy nurturing his fledgling career, and would rather tangle with a Komodo dragon than see her ex-husband again, wasn't likely to do the job.

Finally she shrugged and said, ''Perhaps you should ask Gabriel that question.''

''She probably couldn't face him, if truth be told,'' a pretty woman with long black hair said, filling the silence with an observation Eve couldn't deny. ''I know *I* wouldn't want to, if I were in her shoes.''

The man standing beside her frowned and gave her a not-very-subtle nudge that said plainly, *Button your lip!* Which was a pity. It wasn't the first hint that Marcia had committed some unforgivable sin during her tenure as Gabriel's wife, and Eve itched to know more. But she wasn't about to worm the information out of a stranger. If there was scandal of some sort, decency alone demanded that she learn it from Gabriel.

Choosing her moment when the others were busy helping themselves to *pâté de foie gras,* slices of smoked pheasant, hot crab canapés and other mouthwatering delicacies, she went to find him on the pretext that it was well past Nicola's bedtime.

"I already sent her upstairs with Beryl," he told her, when she finally ran him to earth at the other end of the terrace, "and was just about to rescue you. You've been mobbed ever since you came downstairs. Have you had a chance to eat anything?"

"No, but I'm not really hungry. Gabriel, several people have dropped hints that—"

"Nor I." He hefted a bottle of Perrier Jouet from the nearest ice bucket, and collected two clean glasses. "This is my favorite time of evening," he said, steering her down a shallow flight of steps leading to the gardens. "Let's find a quiet corner where we can watch the moon rise and talk undisturbed. Nobody will miss us."

But it wasn't meant to be. Just then, Thaddo came running after them and informed Gabriel he was wanted on the phone. "I'd better take it," he murmured apologetically. "It could be Marcia, returning my calls at last. Wait for me, *cara,* will you?"

And leave herself open to being collared by another inquisitive guest? Not likely. She was tired of being the *spectacle du jour!*

Catching Thaddo before he returned to the house, she said, "When Signor Brabanti's finished on the phone, please tell him that I'm waiting on the lower lawn."

Pretty lights strung through the branches of the trees illuminated the gravel walk, but Eve was soon hidden by the many shrubs and vines bordering the twisting path, which eventually came out on a narrow plateau overlooking the sea. Tucking her dress around her ankles, she sank down on the grass, in the purple shadow of a tall flowering bush. The relief of escaping the public eye, of not having to justify or defend either herself or Marcia, was huge, and for the first time in what seemed like days, she felt able to breathe freely.

By then, dusk had turned the water to midnight-blue, with the sky a shade paler and pricked with the first faint light of stars. Not a breath of wind stirred the perfumed air. The low boom of the sea washing onto the rocks at the foot of the property masked the hectic buzz of party talk filtering from the house.

If everyone would go home and leave Gabriel and me to enjoy the night alone, it would be perfect, she thought.

But every garden of Eden had its serpent, and if she'd forgotten that, it took only a few words to remind her.

The crunch of footsteps on gravel alerted her to the presence of other people beyond the screen of shrubbery. A second later a woman's voice said, "She seems to have made herself thoroughly at home in his house."

"More likely at home in his bed, if you ask me!" There was no mistaking the Contessa De Rafaelli's plummy tones. "As if she has a hope of becoming the next Mrs. Gabriel Brabanti! At least the other one had a bit of life to her, a smattering of poise and sophistication. But this one... Good God, Iris, she's a dull-as-dishwater little nurse from the American Midwest. What on earth is Gabriel thinking about, treating her as if she's *someone?*"

"Maybe she gives him lots of tender loving care. Heaven knows, he could use some, after what he went through with Marcia."

"*I'd* like to give *her* a bad case of food poisoning," Janine said viciously. "Anything to keep her confined to her quarters, or better yet, send her back where she came from!"

"Well, *he* seems to like her well enough."

"He hasn't left himself with a whole lot of choice, has he? He's saddled with keeping her entertained, so why not entertain himself at the same time, though what they could possibly find to talk about outside the bedroom escapes me."

"I don't know that I agree with you—at least not about their being lovers," the unseen Iris said thoughtfully. "She strikes me as being rather aloof. Somehow, I don't see her being a whole lot of laughs between the sheets."

"She can fake it, if she has to. God knows the rest of us did when we were out trying to snag the right kind of husband."

Initially Eve had felt her face flaming with humiliation at being silent witness to a conversation never meant for her ears, but as it continued, a cold anger swept over her. In her line of her work, she'd faced her share of thugs, thieves, gang leaders and other unsavory members of Chicago's underworld, without flinching. So why now was she cowering furtively behind a bush and allowing two supposedly civilized but highly imperfect strangers to tear her to shreds?

"I might be nothing but a dull little nurse from the boring American Midwest," she declared, rounding the bush so suddenly that Janine and her cohort clutched each other and squealed in alarm, "but I'm smart enough not to risk being sued for slander, which is a damn sight more than can be said of either of you. And I like to think I've got enough class not to badmouth my host's taste in houseguests while I'm stuffing myself with his food, and washing it down with his champagne."

"You were eavesdropping!" Janine squawked in outrage. "How dare you!"

"How dare *you!*" Eve shot back. "You silly, affected woman, just who do you think you are, judging others by your own shabby standards?"

"Well! *Well!*" Eve couldn't be sure, but she thought the *contessa* turned faintly purple. Certainly she looked to be on the verge either of exploding or going into cardiac arrest. "Wait until Gabriel hears about this!"

"Er, maybe it's best if he doesn't, Janine," the one called Iris suggested, closing a restraining hand over her friend's wrist. "Maybe we've said enough and it'd be best if we all forgot this conversation ever took place. I'm sorry if we've offended you, Ms. Cald—Eve.''

''No, you're not,'' Eve snapped. ''You're just sorry you got caught.''

''I'm not,'' Janine declared, her tone as vitriolic as her expression. ''But you certainly will be, my dear. I'm married to the Conte De Rafaelli, which makes me a person of some consequence in these islands, and I'll see to it that many of the doors that might have been open to you before this unpleasant little episode remain very firmly shut in your face.''

Eve shrugged and smiled. ''Given *my* impeccable connections, I doubt that. But even if you're right, I really don't care. What matters to me is that I'm welcome at the Villa Brabanti for as long as I want to stay, and don't you just wish you could say the same?''

''I already can.''

''After tonight's little episode?'' She laughed softly. ''I *really* doubt that, *contessa!*''

''Come away,'' Iris begged, tugging on Janine's arm. ''You're just digging yourself in deeper, don't you see that? If she tells Gabriel about this—''

''She won't,'' the *contessa* sneered, allowing herself to be drawn back along the gravel walk to the house. ''Her pride won't let her.''

Too true! As if she'd accidentally touched something unspeakably foul, Eve gave a shudder, "Ugh!" she muttered, brushing her hands together in disgust.

"My sentiments exactly," a voice from the shadows rumbled, and this time it was her turn to squeal in shock.

"What do you mean by sneaking up like that?" she gasped, when Gabriel emerged from a hidden path between the trees. "You scared me half out of my skin!"

"I wasn't sneaking," he said calmly. "That's never been my style. I merely took a shortcut to meet you as you requested."

"But you *were* eavesdropping!"

"Yes, and finding it *molto difficile* to keep quiet. I was all ready to leap to your defense." His grin flashed in the dusky light. "But *inutile, si?* Not necessary. You were very well able to defend yourself."

But now that the heat of the moment had subsided, reaction set in and left Eve ashamed. "I was very rude to your friends, Gabriel. That's not something I'm proud of."

He deposited the bottle of champagne and glasses on a nearby stone birdbath. "They were mortally insulting to you, *cara mia,* and that's not something I'm about to forgive or forget. What do you suppose started it all?''

''You shouldn't have put your arm around me when I came downstairs. It just gave rise to talk.''

''Should I have done this instead?'' Closing the distance between them, which hadn't been very big to start with, he captured her mouth in a kiss which spoke of a hunger barely held in check.

His lips quested over hers, searching for secrets she'd never intended he should discover. How was she supposed to withstand an assault delivered with such exquisite finesse that she all but melted in a pool at his feet?

He sapped her strength. Left her without the will or sense to keep her lips together. So it was all too easy for him to slide his tongue between them and taste the pent-up desire she couldn't repress. Easier still to stir her to even greater passion by sliding his hands the length of her spine to her bottom, gathering handfuls of her dress en route and pulling her hard against him.

There was no mistaking his arousal, and if he'd continued inching her skirt up her thighs, he'd soon have learned he wasn't the only one aching with unfulfilled longing. The heated rush dampening her underpants betrayed an embarrassing response to his touch.

"Not that, either," she said breathlessly, tearing her mouth free, but while her words denied him, her blood sang with pleasure.

"Why not? Because what others think matters more to you than I do?"

"No," she said, stepping out of his hold, because to be so near him clouded her thinking and blotted out all the many good reasons why they shouldn't allow the passion to run wild between them. "Because I'm afraid you're attracted to me only because I'm not like Marcia."

He smothered a curse. "What the devil does Marcia have to do with any of this?"

"I'm not sure. All I know is that Janine De Rafaelli isn't the only one to imply that Marcia hurt you in some way. And I can't help wondering if you're trying to prove something by turning to someone less...dangerous."

"She didn't hurt me," he said, so coldly furious that Eve shivered. "She didn't possess that power. Instead she embarrassed the hell out of me and dragged my good family name through the dirt."

"How?" Eve demanded, catching at his arm and trying to pull him back to face her when he went to turn away. She hated the closed expression on his face. A moment ago, he'd kissed her as if he could never get enough of her. Now he looked at her as if she were a stranger. "What did she do, Gabriel, that I'm now bearing the brunt of her actions?"

He flung her off. Straightened his jacket sleeve and shot his shirt cuffs into place. "This is neither the time nor the place for such revelation. Please excuse me. I'm neglecting my guests."

"Don't you dare walk away from me as if I'm some impertinent subordinate!" she cried, furious herself. "Damn it, Gabriel, I deserve an answer, and I deserve to get it from you. But if you can't or won't give me one, I'm not too proud to seek it from someone who will."

That stopped him in his tracks! Spinning around, he bore down on her in such a spate of anger that she flinched. "You'll do nothing of the kind! If answers are what you want, meet me in my study when the party's over and I'll give you the whole sordid story. But don't blame me if you don't like what you hear." He let out an exclamation of disgust. "And for God's sake, stop cowering like that! If I managed never to raise my hand to your benighted cousin, you can safely rest assured I'll never strike you, or any other woman for that matter!''

''I never for a moment thought you would, Gabriel,'' she said in a small voice.

But she was talking to the silent garden. Not waiting for her response, he'd disappeared back along the hidden path, as anxious now to escape her company as Janine De Rafaelli had been only minutes earlier.

CHAPTER SEVEN

"THERE was no need to knock," he said, when she entered his study. "You live here. For now at least, this is your home."

A floor lamp in the corner shed a gentle light through the room and showed him sitting in a high-backed wing chair facing the open windows. He'd shed his jacket, pulled loose the knot in his tie and opened the top button of his shirt. A brandy snifter stood on the table at his elbow.

When she didn't reply and instead slipped quietly into the chair next to his, he said, "I thought perhaps you'd changed your mind and weren't coming. It's almost eleven. Our guests left hours ago."

"Nicola needed her ten o'clock feeding."

"And before that? Some people stayed for a cold buffet supper. Why didn't you join us?"

"I…had a headache."

He laughed unkindly. "Is that the best excuse you can come up with, Eve? *I had a headache?*"

"Okay, I wasn't hungry."

"Nor was I. The mere mention of my ex-wife's name is enough to give me indigestion, let alone the idea of rehashing her antics in their every squalid detail. But common courtesy demanded that I not abandon my guests."

"All right, I let you down." She bit her lip and hazarded a glance at him. Had something else happened, or was it really just the prospect of talking about Marcia that left him in such a foul mood? "If you must know, I'd had enough of your friends."

He picked up the snifter and took a mouthful of brandy. He hadn't looked at her once since she arrived, nor did he do so now, preferring instead to stare out at the soft Mediterranean night. What did he see there, she wondered. The blanket of stars spread across the sky, their reflection littering the sea like dancing fragments of crystal, or ghosts of his unhappy marriage?

"You found them universally unpleasant? There wasn't one among them whose company you could tolerate a second time? That puts me in an awkward position. The Ripley-Joneses have invited us to the theater on Wednesday, and the Santoros to dinner next Monday. What am I to tell them? That you'd rather—?"

"Not universally unpleasant, Gabriel. I liked the Santoros very much. The other couple I confess I can't quite place."

"He's in the diplomatic corps and she's the former opera singer."

"Ah, yes. Now I remember. They, too, were very charming."

He permitted himself a small, bitter smile. "Then I've risked little in accepting both invitations? I don't have to worry that you'll embarrass me by walking out in mid-performance on Wednesday, or disappearing halfway through Monday's dinner?"

"Of course not!" Exasperated, she said on a sigh, "Is this why you asked me to meet you here, Gabriel? So that you could pick a fight with me?"

He blinked and turned at last to look at her. "Is that what I'm doing? Forgive me. It's not my intention."

So he said, but his mood change proved otherwise. Her lips still felt slightly swollen, proof that she hadn't imagined his kiss. The imprint of his body lingered on hers, hot and hungry. Yet he spoke like a stranger, his tone chilly, his blue eyes cool. He was fire and ice, his passion swinging from love to loathing in the blink of an eye.

"Then what *is* the matter?" she asked him.

"I've discovered shrugging off the past isn't quite as easy as I'd first thought. The last time I attended the theater with the Ripley-Joneses, Marcia was with me. Very much against her will, as it turned out. She wanted to leave at the first intermission. I refused to accommodate her."

"And?"

He shrugged and swung his gaze back to the window. "Well, you know Marcia. When her demands aren't met, she makes a scene, regardless of where she might be or who might witness her tantrums. I didn't take well to being humiliated in public by the childish antics of a so-called adult and was not, I'm afraid, very kind in expressing my distaste."

"And because I slipped away from tonight's party, you think I'm cut from the same cloth as my cousin? That's a bit of a leap, surely? For a start, nobody but you probably even noticed I was gone. Second, I *did* have a good excuse. The evening lasted much longer than you'd led me to expect, and I'd promised Beryl I wouldn't keep her up too late. But all that aside, Gabriel, after my run-in with the *contessa,* I wasn't in much of a party mood."

"You shouldn't let her get to you. She's not important."

"You shouldn't let Marcia get to you, but even after all these months, you obviously still do."

"She left more lasting scars."

Eve waited a heartbeat, expecting he'd elaborate. When he didn't, she said, "I assume they were caused by something more traumatic than a temper tantrum over a theater engagement?"

"If repeated infidelity falls under such a heading, then yes."

Her mouth fell open in dismay. "Marcia had an *affair?*"

"Several, by all accounts." He shifted the angle of his shoulders. Settled more deeply into the wing chair until all she could see was the thrust of his jaw and nose, and the lock of dark hair falling over his brow. "The first—at least, the first that I was aware of—started four months after we were married. Before that, she merely looked, the way a starving woman might press her face to the window of a restaurant."

"*Several* affairs?" Dismay was turning into shock and, inexplicably, shame. As if, by association, Marcia's disgrace had infected Eve and left her to carry the burden of her cousin's actions. ''Gabriel, I don't know what to say, except that I'm horrified.''

''You're surely not implying this comes as news?''

''Of course it does! I never suspected she'd behave so badly.''

Never? her conscience niggled. *Not even when she announced she was taking a second husband within months of ridding herself of the first?*

Shoving aside the disturbing question, Eve said, ''Why did you wait so long to end things with her?''

''Because divorce isn't something I believe in. And because I blamed myself for her behavior.''

''How could it possibly have been your fault? Did you push her into another man's arms?''

''Not literally, perhaps.''

''What's that supposed to mean?''

''That I realized practically from the start that we were a match made in hell, and made no secret of my feelings. I tolerated her, turned a blind eye to her unhappiness. I gritted my teeth and tried to make the best of a bad situation when what I should have done was swallow my pride, admitted my mistake, and gone about rectifying it in the only way possible.''

"But you didn't seek comfort with another woman."

"No," he said, his eyes still trained on the dark horizon. "I'm sure Marcia regaled you with stories of what a complete bastard I can be, but I do possess some standards. Honoring at least some of my marriage vows happens to be one of them."

"I don't base my judgment of people on what others tell me, Gabriel. I reach my own conclusions and I believe you're painting a much blacker picture of yourself than you deserve."

"I could change your mind on that very easily, Eve."

"How?" she said, the sudden sharp pain in his voice making her heart ache.

Slowly he swung his head toward her again. "What if I told you that when I first heard Marcia was pregnant, I was appalled? I wanted to sever all connection with her, not find myself tied to her forever because of a child conceived out of lust or desperation, or a combination of both."

"I can see how you might feel that way. Every child deserves to be born of love, and it's very sad that so many aren't. But the point is, you didn't turn away from the situation, you accepted it."

"Not gracefully. Plainly put, I did not want this baby. And that was why I didn't make an issue of being there for her birth, or of visiting her sooner. I'd have preferred to ignore her existence."

He spat out the bald truth like a challenge, as if daring Eve to confront a sin of such magnitude and forgive him for it. He'd left it too late. A few weeks ago, she might have been fooled into believing he had no heart, but she knew differently now. "What matters, Gabriel, is that you weren't able to follow through on that resolve. In the end, you couldn't turn your back on Nicola."

"No. In the end, conscience and pity got the better of me, and I took responsibility—but from a distance. I didn't feel like a father. Didn't *want* to feel like one. Couldn't, if truth be known, accept that I'd become one, which is why I eventually decided I had to see my child, before I'd left it too late to learn how to love her." He passed a tired hand down his face. "I know now that if I hadn't met Nicola until she was ten or twenty, I'd have loved her anyway. How could I not? She is part of me."

"Oh, Gabriel," Eve said, with a catch in her voice. "I know you love your little girl. I've watched you with her, and sometimes, the look on your face when you're holding her makes me want to cry.''

''Whatever for?''

''Because I've seen so many babies who've had no one to hold them close. No one to rock them to sleep, or buy them pretty clothes and soft, cuddly toys. I've seen too many with bruises on their little bodies—with broken limbs, or head injuries because some angry man or woman has shaken them until their brains scramble.''

His eyes flew open so wide with shock that his lashes flared like petals around the heart of a flower. *''Per carita,* how do you keep your sanity?''

''Some days, I don't. I leave the clinic and wander for hours along the lakefront, trying to find peace of mind. Sometimes I go nights without being able to sleep because the second I close my eyes, the pictures come back to haunt me and I want to kill the people who commit such atrocities. Other times, I feel so frustrated, so *useless,* that I just want to walk away from it all and never have to look back.

''And sometimes,'' she said, her voice quavering again, more violently this time, ''all I can do is hold a battered child close to my heart, and watch helplessly as his life slips away.''

"*Dio!*" Gabriel surged out of his chair, pulled her to her feet, and wrapped his arms so tightly around her that her ribs hurt. "Nobody should have to endure such torture—never a child, and never a woman like you!"

Clutching his shirt, she muffled her grief against his shoulder. His hand stroked up her back. She was conscious of his fingers lacing through her hair, of his chin resting on the crown of her head. She felt his every agitated breath, and knew he wanted more than to hold her with tenderness. Knew that the passion was running strong in his blood, and the only reason he kept it in check was out of consideration for her fragile emotional state. She had never felt safer or more protected.

"Who looks after you, *cara?*" he asked, his voice rumbling up from the depths of his chest. "Who holds you at the end of the day, and keeps you close in the dark when the nightmares strike?"

"No one," she said.

"Then let me."

"It's not your job."

"Not even if I want to take it on?"

She lifted her face to his, saw with what decisive intent he watched her. "How can you be so sure it *is* what you want, and not just that you feel sorry for me?'' she asked brokenly. ''How do you tell the difference between pity and desire, Gabriel?''

His mouth swept down on hers in soft urgency. ''By this,'' he murmured, allowing just enough space between their lips for the words to escape, ''and by this.''

He pressed her hand to his chest. She felt the invincible strength of him denounced by the erratic thunder of his heart. He was a man of immovable integrity, driven by unimpeachable scruples, yet touched by a capacity for gentleness not often found in other men. To be loved by him would endow a woman with something rare and magnificent.

But to imagine for a second that she could be that woman was courting heartbreak of the worst kind. That he was grateful to her and found her attractive enough, she didn't doubt. But they had no foundation on which to build a grand and lasting passion nor, in the few weeks she'd remain in his house, the opportunity to do so. It wasn't time enough, not by a long chalk. The best—or worst!—they could enjoy was a brief affair. And in her case, it would be the worst. She wasn't very good at short-term flings.

So, ''I'm going upstairs,'' she said, attempting to wriggle out of his hold. ''I'm too far away from the nursery to hear if Nicola wakes, and you're too swept up in the moment to know what you're saying.''

He splayed his hand over her bottom and melded her to him. He was hard, his aroused flesh rebelling against the imposition of clothing coming between them. "But we have unfinished business between the two of us, *cara mia,* and running away will not resolve it.''

''Your imagination's getting the best of you, Gabriel.''

He nudged her hips with his, a flagrantly intimate movement that left her gasping. ''I am not imagining this, *la mia bella,* and neither are you.''

Just for a moment, she allowed herself to wonder what it would be like to lie naked with him; to touch him all over, let him touch her, look his fill, kiss her wherever he chose. To be possessed by him. To feel all that hot, potent strength answering the quivering need of her own body.

Imagination was a powerful thing. A slow and sensuous heat pervaded her limbs. Left her mouth dry and breathless, and the part of her pressed most closely against him wet and eager. Embarrassed, she wrenched herself free and took a step back. "Nevertheless, it'll have to wait for another time."

She was gone before he could recite all the good reasons for her staying. Running like a frightened deer fleeing a hunter. But not so swiftly that he hadn't read the longing in her eyes. Not fast enough that he hadn't seen the hectic flush riding up her throat to suffuse her face, or felt the pebble-hard thrust of her nipples against his chest.

But she was afraid; uncertain that she could trust him. Which left the next move up to him. The question was, with sanity slowing his heart rate to near-normal, and the painful ache in his groin subsiding, how well could he trust himself?

He slumped back into his chair to consider, and reached for his glass. He hadn't offered her any brandy, he realized belatedly. His thoughts had been occupied elsewhere. Now though, in the peaceful quiet of his study, there were no distractions. He could confront his changing perspectives.

Marriage had left him hard and bitter. Dried up whatever tenderness he'd once possessed. Although since his divorce he hadn't gone so far as to deny himself the pleasure of a woman, he never allowed her to touch him, except in the most superficial way. And he never led her to expect more than he was prepared to give.

Funny thing, though. Talking to Eve about Marcia tonight hadn't left the usual disagreeable residue in his mouth. Instead he felt purged. Able to roll the vintage Louis XIII Remy Martin over tongue, and savor the cognac's sweet burn. Able to embrace life again as it should be lived: with the vigor and courage of a man in his prime.

But with Eve? Was he ready for her? His body knew the answer, but his heart...how dependable a guide was it?

He rested his head against the back of his chair and closed his eyes. He could deal with captains of industry, with millionaires and moguls. Could go toe to toe with them, be as hardnosed as it took to win, to be in control of whatever situation they threw at him.

Even Marcia hadn't cost him more than he was able to pay. At the time, his pride might have taken a bit of a beating, but he was too well-armed, his defenses too massively secure, for her to cause any lasting damage.

Eve's vulnerability, though, stripped him bare. Laid waste to his strength. It frightened him because it moved him too much.

He shifted in the chair. Fear was not a familiar or welcome companion. Yet ever since she'd shown up with Nicola, it had made its elusive presence felt in sneak attacks when his back was turned.

He hadn't expected to fall in love with his daughter. Yet she'd taken his heart in her tiny, careless hands and wouldn't give it back. He worried about her. Lost sleep over her.

He hadn't expected to find his thoughts turning to family, to permanence with a woman. Yet the prospect of Eve leaving at summer's end filled him with emptiness, and the idea he'd once harbored, of using her for his own selfish ends, left him feeling physically ill.

He wanted her in the purest sense a man could want a woman. He wanted her and his daughter in his life, for now, for always.

And sitting there stewing about it, examining it from every angle and coming up with the same conclusion every time, was doing nothing to secure either one.

She'd intended to climb into bed, determined that closing her eyes would automatically shut off her thoughts, and that would be enough to still the quiet raging of her body. But peace of mind was not to be had. Midnight chiming from some distant church tower found her pacing restlessly in her lamplit sitting room. Only one thing could silence the expectation strumming along her nerve endings, and when at last she heard the knock at her door, all she knew was a radiant sense of relief that the torture was about to end.

He offered no excuse or apology, but simply strode into the room, locked the door, and leaned with his back against it. He was breathing hard. His tie was gone, and his shirt popped free of its buttons, leaving his bronzed chest bare. His hair was a mess, as if he'd grabbed it by the fistful and tried to yank it out at the roots. His eyes smoldered.

For a long minute, they did nothing but stare at one another in gnawing hunger, each waiting for the other to make the first move. Pent-up longing charged the air like so many lightning bolts run amok. Turned her stomach upside-down. Sent her pulse cartwheeling out of control. Bathed her inner thighs in the fine, sweet dew of passion.

Disconcerted, she tried to draw her gaze away and couldn't. It was as if she were invisibly hot-wired to him. The atmosphere sizzled, the pressure built to unbearable heights. Finally, he shoved himself away from the door and, without a word, took her in his arms and kissed her. She kissed him back and it was all the permission he needed.

She wore only a nightgown and she was glad. Glad that it covered so little, and that he could scatter untamed kisses from her eyelids to her throat. Glad that his hands could wander at will over her shoulders and slide the fabric down her arms until the garment slithered into a cool cotton puddle at her feet.

"I couldn't stay away," he muttered hoarsely.

If, at first, she'd been unsure of what to say, how to react to the situation, now she knew with stunning certainly exactly what she had to do. Weaving her fingers through his hair, she cupped the back of his head and drew his mouth down to meet hers. "I'm glad," she said. "Take me to bed, Gabriel."

He needed no further encouragement. Swinging her into his arms, he covered the distance to the other room in less time than it took the distant church clock to chime the quarter hour. There was no more talking after that, just the rasp of a zipper ripped open with frantic impatience, the rustle and soft thud of clothing falling to the floor.

A shaft of pale moonlight pierced the room, just enough to reveal him to her in all his proud, naked glory. She had seen most of him before, of course, her first week at the villa. But only from a distance, and it seemed a lifetime ago. Now, up close and completely naked, he was magnificent. Awe-inspiring. Larger than life in every respect.

And patient to a fault! Her limited experience with sex had left an impression of something to be dealt with as quickly as possible, and if the end result was one of vague dissatisfaction, well that was just the nature of the beast. Men had orgasms—Will Powers whimpered like a baby when he came—and some women had them, too. But many didn't, and she'd long since accepted that she belonged to the latter group.

But Gabriel didn't know that. Her first clue that he wasn't about to get down to business in a hurry and settle for the merely ordinary was when, instead of climbing on top of her and finding release with all due speed, he instead stretched out beside her and tracked the outline of her mouth with his finger.

The sensory aftershock almost had her gasping aloud. Her skin broke out in a flurry of goose bumps that ran the length of her to gather in a quivering mass in the pit of her stomach.

Next, he explored her ear. That ordinary, taken-for-granted organ bloomed like a flower under his ministrations, demonstrating a capacity for sensation she'd never suspected. She shivered with pleasure as he traced the outer shell, but was completely unprepared for the response he invoked when he leaned forward and dipped his tongue into the inner well.

A bolt of pleasure catapulted straight to the feminine heart of her, causing her flesh to contract in an involuntary spasm. Only when it was much too late to pretend it was accidental did she realize her hands were racing over his torso with mortifying hunger, following the path of dark hair over the muscled curve of his chest, and past the hard ridges of his diaphragm to the flat board of his belly.

Heavenly days, another inch or two and she'd have been fondling his penis—while he was still paying attention to parts of her not just above her waist, but above her neck!

Horrified, she snatched her hands away and clenched her fists against her chest. What had happened to the passive creature who'd had to work so hard to keep her mind on the here and now with Will? Who'd accepted his routine moves with a certain ho-hum tolerance, and offered the same in return?

"I'm so sorry, Gabriel!" she blurted out.

He lifted his head and smiled the smile of an angel—a dark angel, to be sure, with more than a hint of the devil playing around his mouth. "For what, *la mia bella?* For giving, as well as receiving pleasure? Why be sorry about that?"

"Because..." Because what? Because she hadn't asked permission? Because she didn't know him well enough to touch him intimately? If so, what was she doing in bed with him?

"You're nervous," he observed, letting his hand drift down her throat to her cleavage. "Do you have any idea how beautiful it is in a woman, that she welcomes her lover with such shy modesty?"

As he spoke, the pads of his fingers feathered concentric circles around the perimeter of her breast in a rhythm at once so hypnotic and exciting that she thought she'd scream from the sheer tactile bliss of it. "Is that what you are?" she heard herself ask, in a voice she barely recognized it. "My lover?"

"Do you have any doubt?"

She stared at him, the reality of his being there, in her bed, seducing her, still not fully registering. "I'm not sure."

"Then I must convince you. With this...and this..."

His mouth hovered tormentingly over hers, imprinting too brief, too sweet kisses over it, then slid with sudden shocking effect to close over her nipple and capture it lightly between his teeth.

The breath caught in her throat, and she squirmed in a tiny paroxysm of ecstasy so acute that she couldn't contain a moan. As though fearing she might try to escape, he spanned her waist and rolled her onto her back.

"You are very beautiful, *carissima,*" he murmured, his breath whispering over her rib cage, warm and damp and tantalizing.

Yet despite finding herself suspended in a taut web of sensual expectation, she was completely unprepared for his mouth to skim past her navel and settle with stunning impact at the juncture of her thighs. Oh, the blushing heat, then! The instinctive clamping together of her knees, the jolt of embarrassment!

And oh, the shockingly willing relaxation of her thighs as he cajoled her with his tongue! The sultry, simmering escalation of tension as he probed the damp folds of her flesh and with unerring instinct taught her how little she really knew about her body. Her heart missed a beat and then her world quite literally exploded, sending all the bits and pieces of it flying into the stratosphere.

She squeezed her eyes shut and swallowed a scream. Clutched with desperate fingers at his hair, his shoulders. Uttered his name on a high, keening note, begging him to stop...begging him not to...begging for more. And knew, when those same high-flying bits and pieces finally floated back to earth and claimed their place again that, although none were missing, neither did they fit as they once had. She was not the same. She never would never be, ever again.

The realization made her burst into tears.

Dismayed, he lifted his head. *"Per carita, la mia bella, non piangere*—don't cry, my love! We don't have to do this, if you don't want—"

She held open her arms. "Oh, I want!" she sobbed joyfully. "I want very much, Gabriel!"

He inched his body up over hers, and braced himself on his elbows so that he could see her face. "You're sure?" he asked, doubt still painting his voice. "I haven't hurt you?"

"You have freed me," she cried. "And I want you so badly that I ache to feel you inside me."

He drew her hand down between their two bodies and closed it around the silken weight of him. "Do you doubt for a minute that I want you just as badly?"

She shook her head, afraid to speak because the only words bubbling up inside her were *I love you!* and she wasn't so blissed out that she'd allow herself to say the one thing guaranteed to chase him away. Instead she curled her other hand around his neck, pulled his mouth down to hers, and tilted her hips up to meet his.

The tip of his flesh nudged hers and hesitated, and a stillness crept over her; a timeless breath of anticipation. She knew a moment of searing, exquisite tension mingled with a deep and yearning need. Then he guided himself home and the only thing that mattered was how perfectly they came together, how exactly their bodies harmonized.

She felt his breath at her ear, heard the murmured words he uttered in his mother tongue and knew he spoke the language of love as perhaps only an Italian could—with a lilting cadence that matched the increasing rhythm of their entwined bodies.

That, by itself, would have been enough to give a sparkle of stars to her life that would never fade. But Gabriel wasn't a man willing to settle for mere stars. He gave her the moon, bringing it down from the heavens to shower her yet again with a magic beyond anything she'd ever imagined. She soared up to meet it, and knew he flew with her. Knew because she felt the spasms contorting his body even as her own contracted around him. Knew because she felt the hot spill of his seed flooding inside her, and the thudding of his heart at her breast.

She knew because, when at last he lifted his head and looked at her again, she nearly wept at the look of wonder on his face. For the moment, for now, that was enough.

At length, he rolled aside and said regretfully, "I should go. It wouldn't do, I'm afraid, for Beryl to find me here in the morning."

"No, it wouldn't," she said, curbing the urge to cling to him.

He swung his legs to the floor and reached for his clothing. Pulled on his pants and shirt, stuffed his socks into his pocket, and carried his shoes. "You'll join me for breakfast, *cara?*"

"Yes," she said, winding the sheet around herself and following him to the door.

He dropped a kiss on her nose, another on her lips. "Then I'll see you at nine."

It was only two o'clock. Seven long hours before they'd be together again. She didn't know how she stand it.

CHAPTER EIGHT

SOMEWHERE between midnight and dawn, the euphoria vanished and took all her confidence with it. The second her eyes opened to another brilliant Mediterranean morning, doubts bombarded her mind.

What if he was already regretting everything, and wishing he'd never come to her suite? What if he begged off breakfast with her, and every other shared engagement between now and the end of her visit?

Fine thing! she thought, brushing her teeth with a vehemence they didn't deserve. *One night of utter, complete bliss, and I pay for it the next day with my pride in ruins, while he either makes himself scarce or tries to let me down gently.*

But if that was the price, had it been worth it?

She lifted her head and stared at herself in the mirror. Apart from her mouth, bee-stung from his kisses, and her body, aching from his love-making, she did not, at first glance, appear so very different. But closer inspection showed an awareness in her eyes, the kind that came from a woman who'd finally found ultimate sexual and emotional fulfillment.

So, yes, oh, *yes!* Making love with Gabriel was worth every miserable second it might cost her, and she'd do it again in a heartbeat, given the chance.

The question was, would he?

Heart *pit-a-pattering* nervously, she trooped down to face him across the breakfast table, determined to preserve a dignified front, no matter how he received her.

Indifferently, as though to pretend last night had never happened? She could do indifference, and live to talk about it, once the hurting subsided.

Ruefully, with the excuse that he'd had too much to drink and couldn't quite remember all the details, but was terribly sorry if he'd taken advantage of her? She could still do indifference, even if the truth left her crushed to the core.

But if he tried to make a joke of it, although she might succeed in masking her pain on the outside, inside she'd wither and die. To have given him everything she was or ever hoped to be, and have it turned into a laughing matter, would kill her—not literally, perhaps, but she'd be left so emotionally stunted that she'd never recover.

"You're late, *signorina,*" he announced bossily, springing to his feet when she entered the room, fully braced for rejection.

"It's only seven minutes after nine."

"And I've been waiting since a quarter to." Forestalling her attempt to slither into her chair before she collapsed, he swept her into his arms. "Twenty-two minutes you've kept me waiting, and every one torture. How are you this morning, *la mia inamorata?* Wishing you'd never opened the door to me last night?"

Giddy with relief, she sank against him. "Not a chance," she said, lifting her face for his kiss.

He obliged with a thoroughness and enthusiasm that swept away any lingering doubts she might have. Indeed, there was no telling where the kiss might have led if Leola, the maid, hadn't suddenly appeared with toast and coffee.

Schooling his features into something approaching their usual imperturbability, Gabriel ushered Eve to her chair, then took a seat across from her. But she saw the faint bars of color slashed across his cheekbones, the sultry smolder in his eyes, and knew he wasn't nearly as self-possessed as he tried to appear.

"Remind me to keep my distance from you unless there's a locked door between us and the rest of the world," he said, the minute Leola left. "I have a reputation to uphold in this household, and I'm not sure that young woman could cope with the sight of her employer and his lady making love on the breakfast table."

"I'm not sure I like the idea much, either," Eve said, struggling to keep a straight face. "It wouldn't be very comfortable."

He grinned, and it occurred to her he looked younger and more carefree than she'd ever seen him. "Probably not, but you have to admit the idea holds a certain kinky charm!"

"You don't strike me as the kinky type, Gabriel," she replied, smiling despite herself at his use of a word decidedly un-Italian.

"How do I strike you, then?"

She gave the question some thought before answering, "As a man of many layers who doesn't reveal himself easily or quickly. Every day I learn something new about you."

"And you like what you learn?"

Happiness, pure and simple, exploded inside her, effervescent as champagne bubbles. "Very much."

"Same here. You bring light and laughter into my life when I'd given up on both. If Beryl will baby-sit, will you spend today with me? We could do a little sightseeing, if you like.''

''If Beryl's willing to baby-sit, I should go shopping for clothes before our theater date with the Ripley-Joneses. You were right when you told me I'd need to add to my wardrobe. I should have listened to you.''

''I am always right,'' he declared with brash but charming certainty. ''And you should always listen to me.''

''Don't gloat! Nobody needs to hear, *I told you so,* especially not a woman facing a fashion crisis.''

''Then we'll shop together.''

''Oh, right! As if that's how you want to spend your Saturday!''

''It's true I had other things in mind,'' he said, the innuendo behind his words so unmistakable that a flash of heat shot through her. ''But I am a patient man, and a little deprivation now will merely enhance the pleasure to come later. So finish your breakfast, *cara mia,* and let's be off. I will take you to the most elegant boutique Valletta has to offer, and you will model for me.''

But the most elegant boutique was, as she'd suspected, far beyond her means in terms of affordability. "I'm wasting everyone's time coming in here," she protested, dragging her heels as he led her under a canopied entrance and into a shop where even the hushed atmosphere reeked of expense.

"It can't hurt to look," he replied, brushing aside her objections with a careless gesture.

Just then, a salesclerk materialized from the rear of the shop, a tall, elegantly thin woman with black hair swept up in a classic chignon. When she saw Gabriel, her face lit up in a smile that put the sun to shame. *"Signor Brabanti!"*

"Ciao, Rosamunda. Come sta?"

"Bene, bene! E lei?"

"Molto bene, grazie." He cupped Eve's elbow and drew her forward. "Rosamunda, this is my very dear American friend, Signora Caldwell, and we're here to buy a gown. What do you have to show us?"

Rosamunda's glance swept approvingly over Eve. "For such a figure, I have everything!" She nodded to a love seat upholstered in oyster colored silk. *"Si accomodi,* Signor Brabanti, and I will have Filomena bring you a mimosa. *E lei, signorina, da quest parte, per favore—* come with me, please."

She flung back a heavy brocade drapery to reveal a carpeted dais perhaps a foot high, and showed Eve into a large mirrored dressing room equipped with a chair, footstool and small dressing table. "So, *signorina,*" she said, "what is the occasion?"

"A theater date and a dinner party—and I feel it's only right to tell you up-front that one outfit will have to serve for both events, and I can't afford anything too extravagant."

Rosamunda's response was much like Gabriel's. "First we find the gown, then we worry about the price," she decreed, handing her a delicate cotton kimono. "Remove your outdoor clothing and slip into this, then we will look at your options."

The options were beyond gorgeous—and, Eve was sure, so far beyond her budget as to be laughable. But to shimmy into the pleated chiffons, the smooth-as-cream silks, the luscious beaded crepes, was too tempting to pass up. And once she'd been buttoned or laced or zippered into a creation, nothing would do but that Gabriel had to see her in it.

He lounged on the little sofa, enjoying his mimosa, and patiently sat through the fashion show. Finally, when they'd narrowed the choices down to six, his only comment was, "They are perfection on you, every last one! So how many do we take home with us?"

"Only one, Gabriel," she said, thanking providence that she owed nothing on her credit card.

"So choose your favorite."

"Then I think the black lace." At least her black silk pumps with the rhinestone buckles would go with it, and she wouldn't have to spend money on another pair.

"Hmm," he said thoughtfully. "You do not care for the purple?"

"I love them all, but I'll be happy with just the black."

He shrugged, and finished off his wine. "Then it's decided, and we can enjoy a long lunch at a little place I know of down on the waterfront."

"I'd like that," she said, grateful that he didn't embarrass her by offering to pay for her purchase. "I'll be ready in a couple of minutes."

"Take your time, *cara.* Now that you have the gown, there's no hurry. We have the rest of the day to enjoy at our leisure."

What he didn't tell her was that the 'little place down on the waterfront' was his sixty-foot private yacht, and that after they'd been served lunch on the aft deck—an incredible feast of chilled cucumber and mint soup, cold lobster, crusty Italian bread still warm from the oven, and a fruit and cheese plate, all washed down with champagne—he dismissed his crew and conducted her on a tour of the rest of the boat.

It was perhaps one o'clock when they went below deck, and close to four when they emerged into the sunlight again. Three hours of total, utter magic during which she learned that the previous night hadn't been some sort of fluke. He was an inventive, passionate lover and she...oh, any fears she might have harbored that she couldn't respond fully to him were quickly laid to rest.

Her inhibitions melted in the heat of his embrace. His bold seduction inspired her to return in full measure the same overwhelming waves of ecstasy he dealt out to her.

She loved the supple texture of his skin, its taste, its scent. She loved the hissed intake of his breath when she raked her fingernails lightly up his thighs; the shudder that overtook him when she captured his penis between the palms of her hands and held the tip prisoner with her mouth.

"You are the most exciting woman I have ever known," he groaned, the sweat gleaming on his brow, "and you are killing me!"

But most of all, she loved the way their bodies came together, how instinctively they slid into perfect rhythm without either of them having to say a word. The quivering, shimmering acceleration within her body as he brought her to the brink of fulfillment, the shattering destruction of his magnificent strength when he could hold orgasm at bay no longer...they transcended life as she knew it and left her suspended halfway to heaven.

After the third time, he lay beside her, spread-eagled on the rumpled sheets of the master cabin's big bed, and panted, "We were designed for one another, *tesoro*."

She couldn't answer him. Dared not. Because again, the only words filling her love-dazed mind were *I love you!*

He turned his head and looked at her from slumbrous eyes. "I want to sail away with you, find an uninhabited island, and spend days walking naked with you along the sand, swimming naked in the sea. I want to feed you ripe fruit and lick away the juices that run down your beautiful breasts. I want to lie naked beneath the stars with you, stand in the moon-dappled sea, buried tightly within you, with your legs wrapped around my waist, and let the waves serenade us with their song."

He reached across and pressed his hand to her heart. "I want to stop time, *la mia* Eve. It races too quickly toward an ending I'm not ready to face."

And there it was, the one great flaw in their romantic idyll. Already, she had been in Malta over two weeks. In another month, she would be gone.

Rosamunda had promised the black dress would be sent out that afternoon, but when Eve let herself into her suite just before five, she found not one box laid out on her sofa, but six, all bearing the boutique's distinctive logo embossed in silver on the navy lids.

Believing it to be a case of mistaken delivery, she picked up the phone. But, "No mistake," Rosamunda assured her. "They are the gowns you selected as your favorites."

"You must have misunderstood. I can afford only one. I'm afraid I'll have to return the other five."

"Not at all, *signorina,*" Rosamunda said serenely. "Signor Brabanti has taken care of everything."

On the contrary, he'd managed to ruin a hitherto perfect day! Amazed at how easily the sweet aftertaste of love could turn sour, Eve politely hung up the phone, even though what she most wanted was to slam it back in its cradle in a fury, and went in search of Gabriel.

She found him on the terrace, reading the day's mail. On her approach, he glanced up with a smile that would ordinarily have left her melting. But it faded pretty rapidly under the hail of dress boxes, tissue paper and designer gowns she dumped in his lap.

"What the devil—! Have you lost your mind?" he exclaimed, making a grab for the length of beaded cream satin shimmying down his legs.

"Have you lost yours?" she fired back. "Just where do you get off, going behind my back and ordering a load of clothes you know I can't afford?"

"Non importa," he said carelessly. "I have paid for them.

"And you think that makes it okay?"

"Why not? I buy a gift for the woman I admire. Where is the sin in that?"

She wanted to shake him! "A gift is a trinket, a scarf, a photo frame. Six designer gowns—"

"Five," he said, with maddening good humor. "I let you pay for the black lace. The rest are from me because we'll be seen together often, and I want to show you off."

"I'm not a toy poodle, Gabriel, and I'm most definitely not your mistress!"

"Mistress?" He made a pathetic attempt to appear injured. "Where did such a thought come from? You are a woman of great loveliness and deserve to be surrounded with lovely things, *cara mia*."

"I'm sorry if what I wear embarrasses you," she said acidly, "but I'm afraid you'll either have to put up with it, or else leave me home when you go out in public."

"You do not embarrass me," he declared, trying to stuff the gowns back into their boxes. Without much success, she noticed with grim delight. "So much fuss about a few clothes! I thought we'd progressed beyond such foolishness."

"If, by that, you're implying that you're prepared to pay for sleeping with me—"

"Dio, but the woman has a talent for turning a man's words around and biting him with them!" Patience thinning noticeably, he tossed the boxes and their contents to the terrace floor. "Here, take the damned things and throw them over the cliff, if it'll make you feel less insulted."

"I've got a better idea. Send them back to the boutique."

"And be made to look a fool?"

"You're already a fool in my eyes."

He heaved the sigh of a man much misunderstood. "If you will not accept them as a gift from a man to a woman he greatly admires, then consider them the token of a father's gratitude. You brought my daughter to me and have taken the most conscientious care of her, and I am deeply indebted to you on both counts."

"I don't need compensation for looking after a member of my family."

He threw up his hands and let out a stream of unintelligible Italian she swore was enough to turn the air blue. "I am not paying you off, you ridiculous woman! I am trying to show you in what high esteem I hold you!"

"That's not how I see it."

He rolled his eyes. "How is it possible that two women can share a blood tie and yet be so different? Had I presented your cousin with five gowns, her only question would have been, *Why not ten?*"

"Well, if you haven't yet figured out that Marcia and I are about as different as any two people can be, you're more than a fool, you're downright stupid!"

The last of his good humor faded to a scowl. "Have a care, my darling," he advised her silkily. "You're testing my patience. There's a limit to how many slights you may cast at me without retaliation."

"Really?" Although the look in his eyes warned her she was indeed stepping on thin ice, she tossed her head scornfully. "What are you going to do about it, Gabriel, spank me?"

"Tempting though the idea is, no. Nor am I about to offend Rosamunda by returning her merchandise."

"Then you'd better hope the next woman you take to bed wears the same size I do!"

He waited just long enough for the silence to scrape along her nerves and let the inexcusability of such a comment sink home. She'd gone too far. Much too far. And she knew it.

So did he. "I take great exception to that remark, Eve," he said with studied restraint. "I take very great exception to it."

"I'm sorry," she said, embarrassment scalding her cheeks. "I'm afraid I let myself get carried away."

"Perhaps we both acted too hastily," he replied, heading back inside the villa, and she knew he talking not just about the dresses, but the previous twenty-four hours, too. "Perhaps we don't share the same kind of understanding, after all."

A flash of panic seized her. She was angry with him, yes—but not to the point of ending things between them. ''Please don't walk away, just because we disagree on something,'' she begged, the sense that something full of incredibly beautiful promise was slipping between her fingers. ''Please, Gabriel, let's try to work this out.''

He paused just inside the doorway and spared her a glance so impersonal that her blood ran cold. ''I just did—with a marked lack of success, I might add. I am not a man to grovel, Eve, and you appear to be a woman unable to differentiate between a gift and a bribe. That being so, it would seem there's little left for either of us to say.''

She barely saw him for the next three days. He'd send Beryl to the nursery, with instructions to bring Nicola down to visit with him. From her balcony, Eve watched as he strolled in the garden with his daughter in his arms, or sat working on his laptop while she napped on a blanket under the shade of the trees. Twice he took her off in his car and was gone for several hours.

Freed from her baby-sitting responsibilities, Eve did a little sightseeing, swam in the saltwater pool, lounged on the sun-splashed beach, and caught up on her reading. In other words, she tried to fill the empty hours, but found time hanging heavy on her hands, and a cold ache in her heart that no amount of sunshine could ease.

No use telling herself she couldn't possibly have fallen in love with someone she'd known less than a month. Love, she was forced to conclude, wasn't bound by anything as prosaic as time or logic; it had its own set of rules.

The designer gowns, meanwhile, reposed neatly in their boxes, in the corner of her sitting room. Moral scruples notwithstanding, she hadn't been able bring herself to leave them lying crushed on the terrace. Bad enough she and Gabriel were at such serious odds, without the reason for their falling out being left on display to fuel the staff's gossip. The only person she'd confided in was Beryl—and then only partially.

"Well, not that I don't see your point in refusing to accept such an extravagant gift," the housekeeper said, helping her layer the dresses in fresh tissue paper, "but it's a pity to let them go to waste. Couldn't you offer to buy them from him, a bit at a time, love?"

"It'd take me forever. They cost more than I earn in six months," she said.

Then, on the Tuesday afternoon, Gabriel phoned her suite. "Is Nicola still napping?" he asked without preamble.

Juggling the phone, the baby, and a bottle of freshly prepared infant formula, Eve replied, "No. She just woke up and I'm about to feed her."

"Please bring her down to my study when she's finished," he said and hung up.

If it wasn't an outright offer of reconciliation, at least it was better than being treated as if she'd ceased to exist. On a wave of hope, Eve changed into a pale blue sun dress that made the most of her light tan, touched her lips with peach gloss, and presented herself as requested. But she got no farther than the study threshold before Gabriel relieved her of the baby and, with faultless but final courtesy, closed the door in her face.

An hour later, she was summoned downstairs again, this time expecting nothing. And once again was surprised.

"Please come in," he said, ushering her into the room.

He and Nicola were not, as she'd supposed, alone. Another man, a stranger, sat at the big desk, an open briefcase at his elbow.

"I'd like you to meet Gino Cattaneo, an… associate of mine," Gabriel began. "He's agreed to help me locate my ex-wife. Her continued refusal to acknowledge my many messages, or to honor my request for Nicola's medical records, is something I can no longer ignore. I find myself wondering if she's met with some kind of accident."

"Oh, I'm sure not!" Eve exclaimed. "You'd have heard if anything had happened to her."

He permitted himself a small, cool smile. "Not necessarily. I'm not one of *her* favorite people, either."

Eve had little doubt he was making veiled reference to their estrangement, but Gino Cattaneo left her no time to dwell on it.

"Tell me, *signorina,*" he said, pen poised over a pad of lined yellow paper, "have you had any communication at all with your cousin since you arrived in Malta?"

"None," she told him. "I've left several phone messages, but haven't received a reply."

"Would you describe her silence as typical, given the circumstances?"

"I don't know. I've never been in this sort of situation with her before."

"But you have always been close, yes?"

"As close as two people can be, with one living in New York and the other in Chicago. We saw a lot more of each other when we were children."

"Ah, yes," Signor Cattaneo purred, scribbling away. "And speaking of children, how would you explain her apparent lack of interest in her baby? Would you describe it as typical?"

"I'm not sure what you're really asking me, Signor Cattaneo," Eve said brusquely. "If you're suggesting she doesn't love Nicola, you couldn't be more wrong."

"How can you be so sure, *signora?* By your own admission, she's made no attempt to check on her child's welfare."

"For a start, I've contacted her only through her office and she probably doesn't pick up her messages more than once or twice a week."

"Why go through her office? Why not get in touch with her directly? You surely have her cell phone number."

"She's on the road, moving every couple of days or so to another town. Given her extremely crowded schedule combined with the significant time difference between here and the United States, the odds of getting her and not her answering service are slim, even supposing her cell phone's able to pick up a signal from here.

And it has been only a little over two weeks, you know. Not exactly a lifetime.''

''So you can't pinpoint exactly where she might be on any given date?''

''I'm afraid not. But I'm quite certain her office forwards all messages to her and that we'll hear from her before much longer.''

He glanced at Gabriel, lifting his brows as though to say, *She's not much help, is she?*

''*Grazie,* Eve,'' Gabriel said. ''You may leave now, but if you think of anything that might help—''

''I'll be sure to mention it. Would you like me to take Nicola upstairs, too?''

''No,'' he said. ''She's content enough. I'll keep her here with me a little longer.''

The minute the door closed behind her, Gino said, ''Is she telling the truth?''

''I've no reason to believe she'd lie. She's straightforward to a fault.''

''You must admit, though, that it's odd she's as much in the dark as you about the mother's whereabouts?''

''If we were talking about anyone else but Marcia, I'd be inclined to agree. But my ex-wife is an unpredictable creature, as you well know. There could be any number of reasons she chooses to remain incommunicado, and she's smart enough to recognize that her cousin doesn't have her affinity for deception. If she's hatching some sort of scheme, Eve's the last person she'd confide in.''

The lawyer flung down his pen and leaned back in his chair. ''So, where do we go from here?''

''We follow the original plan and try to track her down. There's no love lost between me and Marcia, but she is my daughter's mother. I'd prefer not to wage all-out war until we've exhausted every other avenue.''

''And if we continue to come up empty-handed? If we find her and she still refuses to cooperate?''

He paced to the window and noticed Eve heading down to the pool. She wore a short cover-up over her bathing suit, and had slung a towel over her shoulder. When she'd come to his study, he'd seen the light in her eyes die at his cool reception, and he'd felt a certain grim satisfaction that she wasn't the only one suffering because of their falling out.

But watching her now, he could tell by the discouraged slump of her shoulders that she was miserable, and he was ashamed. Their estrangement had lasted long enough. It was time to make amends.

"Gabriel?" Gino was eyeing him curiously. "Did you hear me? What will you do if Marcia continues along her present path of noncooperation?"

He bent and plucked Nicola out of her playpen. How easily he'd adjusted to her presence in his life, to her physical needs. With what confidence he swung her in the air and cradled her in the curve of his arm, no longer afraid that he might hurt her or drop her. And how emotionally painful it would be to let her go when they time came for her leave him.

"If that happens, Gino," he said, and there was a catch in his voice when he spoke, "then we do whatever we have to do to protect my daughter's interests."

CHAPTER NINE

THEY were late arriving at the Manoel Theatre on Wednesday evening, which left little opportunity for pleasantries with their hosts.

"Don't blame Eve," Gabriel said, shaking hands with Henderson Ripley-Jones. "She was ready on time, but I...detained her."

In fact, at his request, they'd left the villa over two hours before and driven down the coast to a quiet country inn for a light pretheater dinner.

"I've missed you," he told her, after they'd been seated at a table in the courtyard, and served a platter of antipasti accompanied by a bottle of Pino Bianco.

"I'd never have guessed," she replied, fiddling with the black beaded evening bag on her lap.

"I know, and I'm sorry I shut you out." He'd shrugged and aimed a smile in her direction, but she hadn't noticed. "Can we start over?"

She stared out at the sea, her lashes forming a long, dark curve against the early evening sky. "Is there any point? We obviously don't see eye to eye on the things that matter."

199

"Cara," he said, "we had a misunderstanding over a gift. Let's not allow something so trivial to come between us."

"You call the last three days of your acting as if I didn't exist, trivial?" The wounded look she turned on him almost brought him to his knees. "I was angry with you on Saturday, with good reason, Gabriel, and said things I probably shouldn't have. But you wouldn't accept my apology, and you've done nothing but punish me ever since. Do you have any idea how much that hurt?"

"If I didn't before, I do now. I have only to look in your eyes to see the pain I've caused you." He grabbed her hand and refused to let her pull away. "Look, I made a mistake, Eve, but I'd like the chance to fix it, if you'll let me."

She averted her gaze.

"Please! We've come so far in such a short time. You've changed my whole life. I've known more happiness in the last two weeks than I have in years. Throw away the gowns if you must, but please don't throw us out with them."

Defeated, she sighed. "You make it hard for me to refuse you."

"Does that mean I'm forgiven?"

"This time, perhaps," she allowed, just the faintest hint of a smile playing over her mouth and taking the sting out of her reply, "but it'd better not happen again."

"What can I say? I'm half-Sicilian, and swallowing my male pride doesn't come easily. Ask anyone who knows me." Making a shameless play for sympathy, he shot her a soulful glance from beneath his lashes. "But you're the only one who can break me of the habit. Abandon me now, and I'll remain a hopeless case of Italian *machismo* at its most annoying."

She'd tried, but she hadn't been able to hold back her laughter, and he'd known then that they were on solid ground again. "That's a line and a half, if ever I heard one! Are you sure you're not part Irish, too?"

"I'll be anything you want me to be, cara. Just don't give up on us."

"I don't like fighting with you, Gabriel," she said, sobering.

"Nor I with you," he murmured. "I'd much rather make love. Do you suppose we could forget we have a theater date and persuade the innkeeper to rent us a room for the night?"

"No, I certainly don't, and you should be ashamed for even suggesting such a thing!"

"Then how about we cut things short here and spend a little time alone before heading back to the city? Better I *show* you how much I've missed you, instead of just talking about it."

She gave the proposal serious consideration, tilting her head to one side and tapping her fingernail against her front teeth, before finally saying, "I think that's an excellent idea. Let's do it."

It had been a disastrous idea! For the two of them to be alone in the car, on an isolated stretch of road, with dusk closing all around them; for him to hold her again, to inhale the scent of her hair, feel her skin warm and responsive to his touch, taste her mouth, and be satisfied with just that, was nothing short of torture.

"We can't," she whispered, the shudder racing over her body telling him how dangerously close to succumbing to temptation she was when he found the slit in her skirt and ran his hand up her thigh. "Not here, Gabriel, and not now."

No use arguing the point when she was indisputably right. To renege on their date with the Ripley-Joneses was unthinkable. So, while she straightened her dress, fixed her hair, and repaired her makeup, he'd climbed out of the car and paced to the edge of the cliff, willing the painful ache in his groin to subside.

It hadn't been easy. Even now, as they wove a path among the crowd of theater-goers milling outside the Manoel's entrance, the recollection of how she'd looked, applying lipstick to her delectable mouth, made him hard all over again.

Oblivious to his discomfort, Marjorie Ripley-Jones gave him a hug, then kissed Eve on both cheeks. "It's lovely to see you both again. I hope you enjoy tonight's performance, Eve. They're doing *Carmen* this month, and even people who aren't all that fond of opera usually find this one tolerable."

"I'm sure I'll love it," she murmured, clearly smitten by the theater's old-world decor. "What a magnificent place this is!"

"Isn't it, though?" Tucking her arm through Eve's, Marjorie led the way inside. "It was built in 1731 by the Knights of Malta, and is reputed to be the oldest theater in Europe still in operation. We'll take you on a tour afterward, if you like, but right now we'd better make our way to our box. Latecomers aren't allowed inside, once the performance starts."

Gabriel could see that Eve was stunned by the sumptuous interior of the auditorium, and small wonder. Even he, who'd seen in countless times, never failed to be impressed. The painted domed ceiling alone was remarkable, and never mind the ornately gilded boxes, red-carpeted aisles and plush green velvet seats.

As usual for the Ripley-Joneses, who did everything in style, a perfectly chilled magnum of Bollinger *Grande Annee* stood ready on a table at the rear of their box. "Opera goes down much more smoothly with the help of good champagne," Henderson said, filling four glasses and passing them around.

The lights dimmed just then, a hush fell over the audience, and the orchestra blasted into the stirring intro to *Carmen* with an enthusiasm and skill that would have made Bizet proud. A short time later, the curtain rose and the action unfolded in all its colorful, impassioned melodrama.

For the next three hours, Eve watched the action on stage, and Gabriel watched her, captivated. She leaned forward intently in her chair, her hands clasped at her throat, her lower lip caught between her teeth. Her breasts rose and fell beneath the black lace of her gown, her skin glowed soft as pearl in the subdued reflection of the stage lights.

Her champagne remained untouched and he knew that although she sat close enough for him to reach out and touch her, in spirit she was far away from Malta, her heart and soul engaged in the fate of the wild Spanish gypsy spiraling ever closer to her dark end.

He heard her sudden intake of breath during the last tragic scenes, noticed the single tear roll down her cheek. He saw how spontaneously she rose to her feet at the final curtain, how wildly she applauded.

Suddenly, as though sensing he was watching her, she tore her attention from the stage, and turned her head. Their glances collided, and the clamor and crowd surrounding them melted away until there were just the two of them, locked in their own private world. In that moment, he knew with absolute certainty that he wanted her to be a part of his life forever.

This, he thought, is how it should be between a man and a woman—this sense of union that requires neither word nor action to be understood.

''We've reserved a table in the courtyard for a late supper,'' Henderson told her, as they left the box and joined the throng streaming from the auditorium. ''It's the done thing after a performance at the Manoel. How'd you enjoy the opera?''

The smile she turned on him was so luminous that Gabriel knew a moment of irrational jealousy. ''It was *wonderful!*'' she exclaimed, breathless with pleasure. ''Beyond anything I've ever experienced before, and I can't thank you enough for inviting me to join you!''

Henderson and Marjorie beamed at one another and shot him a telling glance over her head, one that said all too clearly, *You'd never know she was related to Marcia, would you?*

Acknowledging the unspoken message with a nod, he slipped his arm around her waist and hugged her to his side, not giving a damn that such a public demonstration of affection would stir up a fever of gossip.

''I'm glad you're having such a good time,'' he told her, bending close to her ear to make himself heard over the noise, ''but I'll be gladder still when I have you to myself again. This evening doesn't end here.''

''You've worked a miracle on Gabriel,'' Marjorie confided, smiling at Eve through the mirror above the vanity, when the two of them visited the ladies' room prior to leaving the theater. ''I've never seen him so...well, I suppose 'happy' is the only word, although it doesn't really do him justice. The change in him is quite remarkable. And if you don't mind my saying so, you look pretty radiant yourself.''

Eve could have answered, *That's because I've fallen madly in love with him!* She made do with a heartfelt, ''Thank you! Malta agrees with me, I guess.''

''He was always a bit of a loner, you know, even before his disastrous marriage—'' Marjorie stopped and clapped an appalled hand to her mouth. ''Oh, forgive me, Eve! You're so different from his ex-wife that I'd quite forgotten she's your cousin.''

''Well, at least something good resulted from the marriage,'' Eve said, steering a neutral course out of long-standing loyalty to Marcia. ''Nicola is a sheer delight.''

''Oh, indeed! I don't know how Gabriel's going to cope when it's time for her to go home again, but he's a strong, resourceful man. I'm sure he'll find a way.'' She shot Eve a coy glance. ''Perhaps you'll take his mind off his loss.''

''You forget, I'll be leaving with Nicola. She's the only reason I'm here to begin with.''

"But it doesn't automatically follow that she'll be the reason you have to leave, my dear. There are other...alternatives."

Were there? Was it possible that what had started as a favor to Marcia could end up being Eve's passport to a future with Gabriel Brabanti, a man who could take his pick of any woman in the world, but who appeared to want her?

The outer door opened just then and the Contessa De Rafaelli, decked out in flame-red taffeta, paraded into the room. "I thought it was you, Marjorie," she declared, in her usual penetrating tones, "but I was sure I must have been mistaken."

"Oh, hello, Janine. Why's that?" Marjorie replied coolly.

"You're not with your good friends, the Graysons. Don't you usually invite them to join you at the opera?"

"Not always. We have a number of other friends whose company we also enjoy."

"Really?" The *contessa's* eyes passed over Eve much the way a broom might sweep aside a dust bunny. "I must not have noticed them tonight."

Turning from the mirror, Marjorie took Eve's hand. "Since you know Gabriel so well, you surely remember his lady friend, Eve, don't you,

Janine?'' she inquired, the reproof in her tone unmistakable.

''How could I possibly forget, after our last encounter?'' Janine fixed Eve in a cold, malicious smile. ''What a sweet little dress, dear. Did you make it yourself?''

''No.'' Eve felt the flush invade her cheeks, and hated it. Not for the world would she give a woman like Janine De Rafaelli the satisfaction of knowing her nasty little barb had found its mark.

''Did you make yours, Janine?'' Marjorie asked, giving Eve's fingers a squeeze.

The contessa let out a peal of laughter. ''When I can well afford to pay a seamstress? Don't be ridiculous! Why on earth would you even ask?''

''I thought perhaps you were trying to pass yourself off as another Carmen,'' Marjorie cooed sweetly. ''Come along, Eve. Gabriel won't appreciate my keeping you here when I know he's panting to have you all to himself again.''

They found Henderson among the crowd on the street just outside the theater entrance. ''Gabriel's gone to get his car,'' he announced. ''We're parked pretty close by but because you were a bit late getting here, his is some distance away, so I promised him we'd stay with Eve until he gets back.''

It was almost midnight, and the Ripley-Joneses had been more than kind. Eve wasn't about to trespass further on their good nature. ''You'll do no such thing. I'll be perfectly fine on my own.''

''Of course we'll wait,'' Marjorie said. ''We're not leaving you out here alone at this hour of night.''

''I'm hardly alone.'' Laughing, she turned to Henderson. ''Please tell your wife not to worry, and take her home. And thank you both again for an absolutely fabulous evening.''

He took her hand. ''It was our pleasure. Are you sure you don't mind—''

''Most definitely.''

''We'll see you again soon,'' Marjorie whispered, giving her a hug. ''And pay no attention to Janine de Rafaelli. She's nothing but a spider!''

And the spider hadn't done with her yet!

''A scandalous affair, if you ask me!'' There was no mistaking the lacquered malice in the *contessa's* voice, coming from somewhere close behind Eve, as the Ripley-Joneses's car drove away. ''The ex-wife's cousin—another grasping American, if you please!—trying to worm her way into the heart of our wounded European aristocrat, Gabriel Brabanti. Poor man! Talk about out of the frying pan and into the fire! I really thought he had more sense than to be taken in by…''

Ears burning, face flaming, Eve stepped off the curb, prepared to hike back to the villa on foot rather than subject herself to another round of humiliation at the hands of Janine De Rafaelli. But she'd taken no more than three paces when a collective gasp of horror went up from those standing nearest to her, and a car, brakes screeching through the night, swerved to a stop mere inches from where she stood pinned in the bright arc of its headlights.

A second later, Gabriel sprang from the driver's seat, his face ashen. *''Dio!''* he uttered hoarsely, so agitated he grabbed her shoulders in a painful grip and practically shook her. ''I almost killed you! In God's name, *cara,* what prompted you to walk out into the road like that, without looking first?''

''I wasn't thinking,'' she said, the adrenalin shooting through her bloodstream draping her in an unnatural calm. ''I forgot you drive on the left over here. I'm sorry. I didn't mean to scare you.''

Anxious onlookers closed in on them in a dizzying confusion of texture and sound, the men starkly elegant in black tie, the women unmindful of expensive silk hems swirling in the dust.

"That was a close call!"

"Is she hurt—?"

"I don't think the car actually hit her, but she looks ready to pass out."

"Chiami un'ambulanza!"

"I'm a doctor. Let me take a look at her."

"I don't need an ambulance or a doctor, Gabriel," she whispered urgently, lifting her face to his. "I just need to get away from here. Please!"

He took a long hard look at her before nodding agreement. "She's fine," he told the crowd, bundling her into the car. "A little shaken up, but not hurt. *Grazie!* Thank you for your concern."

He pulled the car into the stream of traffic and, before long, the bright street lights gave way to the moonlit stretch of coast road heading out of the city. Eve huddled in her seat, delayed shock leaving her trembling like a leaf.

Noticing, Gabriel flicked a dial on the dash that sent a current of warm air fanning around her ankles. "Are you going to tell me what really happened, *cara?"*

"I already did," she said, teeth rattling despite her effort to stop them.

After a series of swooping curves, the road straightened out into a long, flat stretch. He pressed down harder on the accelerator. The green glow from the instrument panel outlined his profile in grim relief.

"I don't think so," he said flatly. "The woman I know doesn't give in to suicidal impulses without good reason." He waited a nanosecond. "Did someone push you?"

"Not in the way you mean." The *contessa,* she realized, hadn't been among those shocked into expressing concern for her safety, which was a wise decision on her part. Given the chance, Eve might have scratched the woman's eyes out, and wouldn't that have made for colorful headlines in tomorrow morning's newspaper!

"Then how? Stop talking in riddles and explain yourself!"

"Your dear friend, the Contessa De Rafaelli, if you must know," she said, sufficiently irked by his imperious tone to toss caution to the winds. Let him find out what kind of friends he had! "She doesn't like the idea of you being seen in public with me and voiced her disapproval for all to hear."

"And you allowed *that* to make you risk being killed or maimed for life?"

"You didn't hear what she said."

"So tell me, word for word."

"No," she said, her rush of anger subsiding as quickly as it had arisen. "It's not worth repeating."

"If it caused you the kind of distress that had you almost under the front wheels of my car, it most certainly is! So tell me yourself, or I'll wring the words out of her, one pain-filled syllable at a time." He drew in a hissing breath. "On the other hand, perhaps it's better that I don't know, or I might be tempted to wring her miserable neck instead, and I hardly consider her worth serving time for."

"Exactly," Eve said. "So let's just forget it."

"Oh, I won't do that," he said grimly. "I've known Pierone since we were both boys in school, and I'd hate to lose his friendship, but I'll make a point of avoiding his wife in future. And if he asks me why, I'll tell him."

"There's no need. I won't be here all that much longer."

"Are you so sure of that, *cara?*" he asked, reaching for her hand.

More than the car heater filled her with warmth at that. "No," she said, suddenly compelled to speak honestly. "I'm not sure of anything since I met you."

"Then let us find a way to rid you of your doubts." Without taking his eyes off the road, he raised her hand to his lips. "When I'm looking to escape the frantic pace of life in Valletta, I go to my retreat on Gozo. It's a quiet and simple place, no servants to speak of, little in the way of luxury, but very beautiful and very peaceful. I would like to take you and Nicola there for a few days. If you agree, we can leave in the morning and stay until Monday."

Four whole days without fear of running afoul of Janine De Rafaelli's vicious tongue? "It sounds heavenly!"

"Then it's arranged. We'll leave early and not come back until it's time to dress for dinner with the Santoros."

With that to look forward to, it didn't matter that when they arrived at the villa, she went to her suite alone.

"I would come with you," he said, snaring her by the waist when she reached the foot of the stairs, "if it weren't that already it's past midnight."

"And that Beryl's baby-sitting and sneaking you past her would be next to impossible." She looped her arms around his neck and leaned into his solid male warmth. "I rather think she'll be glad to be rid of us for a few days. We've created enormous upheaval in her routine."

"And in danger of giving her a heart attack if she catches us like this," he said hoarsely, sliding his hands to her hips and pulling her close. "Pack only a swimsuit, cara. I intend to see a lot of you, over the next few days."

She inched up one stair so that she was more or less at eye level with him. He ran a slow finger from the juncture of her thighs to her throat. A tremor jolted from the pit of her stomach to land with seeping warmth between her legs, making her gasp.

He brought his lips to hers. "Go, before I embarrass myself," he murmured, breathing the word into her mouth.

She backed away, her gaze locked with his in quiet joy. She had never felt so alive. Never so filled with hope.

She and Nicola joined him in the dining room just after eight the next morning. "We're packed and ready to go."

"Take your time over breakfast," he said, bending over the back of her chair to plant a kiss on the crown of her head, and another on his daughter's. "I have a couple of phone calls to make, but we'll be out of here before ten."

Once in the library, with the door closed, he picked up the phone and dialed. It rang twice at the other end before it was answered. "Anything new?" he asked.

"Not a word," Gino Cattaneo replied. "It looks as if we're going to have play hardball, Gabriel."

"Do what you have to do, then. I'll be away until after the weekend, but you can reach me through my cell phone if you need to get in touch."

"And your daughter? Her doctor is pleased with her progress?"

"Delighted," he said. "She's thriving, and I intend to keep it that way."

Reaching Gozo involved a twenty-minute ferry ride, and a drive lasting another half hour. This island, Eve saw at once, was quite different from Malta's. Much greener, much more rural and unspoilt, with flat-topped hills, densely cultivated land, and rugged cliffs knifing down to beautiful secluded inlets.

Gabriel's retreat turned out to be a restored farmhouse set on several acres, overlooking a peaceful valley to the east, a view of the sea to the west, and approached by a long, dusty track barely wide enough to accommodate his black SUV.

Wild poppies spilled around the perimeter of the house itself, but a neatly tended garden to one side was planted with tomatoes, lettuce and cucumbers. A grape arbor, heavy with clusters of ripe fruit shaded a small courtyard, and a small herb patch outside the kitchen filled the air with the scent of thyme and rosemary.

"Leave everything for now. I'll get the luggage later," Gabriel said, hoisting Nicola onto his shoulder and offering Eve his other arm. "Come inside and meet Fiora."

As they approached the house, a fat tabby cat lazing in the sunshine on the front step rolled onto her back and squirmed in anticipation of a tummy rub. "Move over, Leila," he scolded. "Can't you see I've got both hands full?"

He pushed open the door with his foot and gestured for Eve to precede him inside. She found herself in a low-ceilinged room, with a stone floor covered by a woven rug, and bare whitewashed walls. A staircase rose up at one end, and an ancient fireplace stood at the other, unused on such a hot summer day. Instead the air was pleasantly cool.

"That's because the walls are nearly a foot thick," Gabriel told her, when she commented. "Just as well. We don't have air conditioning here."

The furniture was sparse but comfortable: a long couch with deep padded cushions, two armchairs, the kind a person could sink into and feel as if she were being held in a mother's lap, a low table on which sat a pottery jar filled with flowers, and another, smaller table between the two chairs. A double pedestal desk, three shelves loaded with an assortment of books, a small stereo unit, and a couple of reading lamps completed the decor. "Keep going," Gabriel urged, nodding to a door set in the middle of the fourth wall.

This led to a kitchen-cum-dining room at the back of the house. A scrubbed wooden table surrounded by four ladder-back chairs with rush woven seats took up much of the floor space. A wonderful old kitchen dresser filled one wall, its shelves crammed with mismatched crockery. Braids of garlic and dried peppers hung beside the open window, huge stone crocks stood in the corner, with, above them, a selection of copper pots and pans suspended from an iron rack.

From what she could see, painted wooden cupboards lined one wall of the scullery beyond, with the rest of the area taken up by a shallow sink and counter, an electric stove, refrigerator, and old-fashioned washing machine. A woman somewhere between seventy and a hundred—Fiora, she soon learned—stood at an ironing board, smoothing a heavy flatiron over white cotton sheets.

She spoke no English, so Eve wasn't able to follow the conversation taking place between her and Gabriel, but she saw the way the servant's dark, impassive eyes looked her over from head to foot, and had the feeling she didn't meet with much approval. But when the old woman caught sight of Nicola, her face split in a near-toothless smile. The flatiron and sheets were left to fend for themselves, and she held out her leathery brown arms, crooning something in Maltese which Eve took to mean, What's her name?

"Nicola," Gabriel replied. then rattled off a few more words to introduce Eve.

"Ha!" She dismissed Eve with a curt nod.

To her shame, Eve wasn't above hoping Nicola would spit up on the old crone, but the baby lay in her arms, contented as a well-fed kitten. "Well," Eve said brightly, turning to Gabriel, "since I don't seem to be needed here at the moment, why don't I help you unload the car?''

''Don't take offense at Fiora. She's old and set in her ways,'' he said, slinging an arm around her shoulders as they made their way back to the SUV. ''Marcia left a bad taste in her mouth, but you'll win her over in no time at all.'' He stopped behind the grape arbor and tilted her mouth up to meet his. ''And why are we here, anyway, if not for this?''

The kiss was delicious, and went a long way to soothing her ruffled feelings, but one question refused to go unanswered. ''Does she live at the house?''

He shook his head. ''She stays with her daughter in the village just down the road. And if you'd rather not have to deal with her, I'll tell her to stay away while we're here.''

''No, don't do that. I don't want to hurt her feelings.'' She shrugged and laughed. ''If I can survive the contessa's unbridled malice, I can survive Fiora.''

Before she left for the day, Fiora had spread a checkered cloth over the outside table, and left a simple supper of sun-warm tomatoes, cucumbers, olives and freshly caught sardines drizzled with olive oil and oregano, accompanied by a loaf of crusty white bread and sweet butter, with fig tarts for dessert. When Eve came downstairs just after eight, Gabriel was there ahead of her, opening a bottle of wine.

To her surprise, his hair was damp and he'd changed from the khaki shorts he'd worn earlier to a pair of cream slacks and a navy polo shirt. Changing into clean clothes she could understand—they'd spent the afternoon on the beach and done more than a little rolling around on the sand. But that he'd bathed, too? There was only one bathroom in the farmhouse, and she'd spent the last half hour in there. Alone.

"Feel better?" he asked, greeting her with a kiss.

"Much," she said. "A cool bath was just what I needed." She touched his hair, and yes, it was damp. And he smelled of shaving soap and shampoo. "But where have you been, that you're all spruced up? Not that I'm complaining, you understand. You clean up very nicely!"

He ran his hand up his jaw, testing its smoothness. "I boiled water, to shave at the scullery sink, and used the garden shower."

"I didn't realize there was a shower out there."

"It's for rinsing off after swimming in the sea, and hooked up to cold water only which is a good thing.'' He curved one finger inside the elasticized band of fabric holding up her strapless dress. ''Too many evenings with you looking like this, and I'm going to be spending most of time out there. What do you call this thing, anyway?''

She looked down at the long, loose garment, unsure how to answer. She'd made it herself, last summer, from yards of semitransparent Indian cotton she'd bought at a discount outlet. As a fashion statement, it fell sadly short of the mark, possessing neither style nor sophistication, but it was cool and comfortable during Chicago's humid summer nights, and she'd thrown it in her suitcase, thinking it might serve equally well here. ''It's a sarong of sorts.''

''It's a crime against humanity, you mean! How's a man supposed to be satisfied with ordinary food when his woman looks good enough to eat?'' He blew out a sigh and swiped a hand across his brow. ''How about I pour us both a glass of wine, and we sit and admire the sunset while I compose myself?''

''The sun set about two hours ago, Gabriel!'' she said, laughing.

Indeed, the only light came from dozens of tea candles flickering in jars of water, scattered at random around the courtyard and under the grape arbor. A far cry from the elegant sterling gracing the dining room in the Villa Brabanti, to be sure, but the effect was as charming as if a host of fireflies danced in the night.

"I hadn't noticed," he said. "I've been too busy watching you." He handed her a glass of wine and sat down next to her on a crudely fashioned bench made from the twisted branches of some kind of tree. "So, what do you think of my simple country retreat?"

"It's charming! Every bit as peaceful as you said it would be. I can see why you'd want to escape here, every chance you get."

"Marcia hated it."

Eve laughed again. "She would! Not enough happening to keep her entertained. She's a city woman to the core, never happier than when her high heels are clattering down the marble floor of the nearest shopping mall. Barefoot in the sand just isn't her cup of tea."

"But you didn't seem to mind it." He looked down at her painted toe nails peeping from beneath the flowing hem of her dress.

Following his glance, she saw that against their silvery-pink sheen, the skin on her feet took on the color of wild honey. Many more days like today, and she'd be tanned all over.

"I didn't. I loved it—loved being with just you and Nicola."

"She was a pretty happy baby today, don't you think?"

"Yes. And she went to sleep tonight like an angel, probably because..." She stopped, her throat aching suddenly and her voice trapped with the threat of tears.

Probably because she felt for the first time in her short, sweet life like a normal baby, wrapped in the love of two doting parents....

Except Gabriel was the only one entitled to that description, even if, to an outsider looking in, they'd appeared like a happy family. While Eve had folded towels and prepared the playpen into a makeshift crib in the smaller of the two upstairs rooms, Gabriel had sprawled on his back on the narrow bed and played with Nicola, tossing her in the air, tickling her, blowing kisses on the soles of her feet, and finally laying her on his bare chest with her little face pressed close to his.

The room had been filled with her squeals of glee and hilarious little belly laugh, and watching them, Eve's heart had given a lurch. She'd yearned to gather them both to her; to be part of the laughter and yes, part of the tears that might fall sometimes. But she didn't belong, not really. Nicola wasn't hers, and Gabriel certainly wasn't.

"Probably," she said, eyeing him with mock severity when she trusted herself to speak again, "because you wore her out with your antics!"

He took her hand. "You really love her, don't you?"

"Of course I do!" she whispered thickly.

He tightened his fingers around hers and pinned her in his direct blue gaze. "Tell me, *la mia bella,* is there any chance you might one day learn to love me, as well?"

CHAPTER TEN

HE SAW how he'd shocked her with his question. Her eyes flew wide and her delectable mouth dropped open, tempting him to cover it with his and thus delay the rejection he'd no doubt invited.

"Love you?" she said faintly, the glass of wine in her hand tilting dangerously and almost spilling on her dress. *"Love you?"*

He removed the glass and set it on the rickety table beside him. "Am I so impossible a man that such a notion is distasteful to you?"

"Impossible?" she whispered, in that same dazed fashion. *"Distasteful?"* Her hand drifted up, caressed his jaw. "Oh, Gabriel, if you only knew!"

"I know that you have stolen my heart," he said, speaking with difficulty around the tightness in his throat. "I know that I don't want to see you leave when your time here comes to an end. I cannot imagine how I'll live in my house in Valletta, or here in this cottage, without the sound of your laughter haunting me."

Too restless to remain seated, he sprang up from the bench and paced over the flagstone terrace. "This time limit hanging over our heads is driving me mad. I don't want to be counting the days 'til you leave me. I want to look forward to the hours, the years, to be lived with you by my side."

"What are you saying?" Her eyes, huge as deep gray pools, tracked his every step.

He came back to where she sat, her spine straight as a ruler, the fabric of her dress falling gently over her slight curves. Dropping down beside her on the bench again, he caught her hand. Turned it over and studied her palm for a long time, before raising his gaze to meet hers.

"That I want more," he said huskily. "That I want forever. I'm asking you to marry me, Eve."

"*What?*" she gasped, on an explosion of soft, incredulous laughter.

"Marry me," he said again. "If not for my sake, then for Nicola's. Help me give her the kind of home she deserves, so that when she comes to visit, she knows she belongs and is loved."

"No...." Her answer floated on the soft night air with quiet finality. She pressed the tips of her fingers to his mouth and shook her head so that the candlelight caught the sun-streaked strands of her hair and turned them to shimmering gold. *"No!"*

At that, a terrible black emptiness spread through him. "I ask for too much, then?"

"You don't need to bribe me to love you for anyone's sake but your own, Gabriel," she told him reproachfully. "I already love you for yourself. I think I have loved you since the moment I first saw you." A sigh shook her, making the folds of her dress stir and shift softly. "But to marry you...?"

He captured her other hand also and squeezed them both between his, so hard he could feel each delicate bone in her fingers. "Why not?" he said, hope flaring within him like fire. *"Why not?"*

She gave his question long thought before answering, "You've told me often enough that I'm not like Marcia."

"I wouldn't be asking you to become my wife, if you were, *tesoro!*"

"But I'm not as sophisticated as your friends, either. I like nice things, of course—pretty clothes, a comfortable home, the occasional night on the town—but I don't need to be constantly entertained. I'm happy living a quiet life, most of the time." The look she turned on him was heartbreaking in its candor. "I'm a house-in-the-suburbs-with-children kind of woman, Gabriel, not a blue-blood socialite."

"And I'm a man who loves you."

"We're too different."

"We're the same in the things that count."

"Janine De Rafaelli doesn't think I'm good enough for you, and she's probably not the only one of that opinion."

"Who's Janine De Rafaelli?" he muttered, letting go of her hands to cup her face and draw her closer. "And who the devil cares what she thinks?"

Her mouth trembled under his and he felt her pushing weakly at his chest. "People will say it's too soon, that you're on the rebound."

"What you say is all that matters to me," he said, and kissed her again, deeply and at length.

She tasted of passion and goodness, surely two of the most desirable qualities any woman could possess. But both rarely occurred together, and he considered himself among the most fortunate of men that he'd found them in her.

"I know you have a life in Chicago, a career, friends, family," he said when, breathless, they drew apart. "I know I'm asking you to give all that up for a man whose track record as a husband leaves much to be desired, but—''

''Gabriel,'' she interrupted.

''But there's a difference,'' he rushed on, feeling as if he were trying to hold water in his hands and was helpless to stop it leaking away. He was not used to feeling helpless. ''I did not love Marcia—''

''Yes,'' she said.

''No, I did not! What I feel for you is as different from the attraction that drew me to her as night is from day. It doesn't begin to—''

''Yes, Gabriel,'' she said again.

He stared at her, confused. ''Why do you keep saying that?''

''Because I thought it was what you wanted to hear.'' She reached up and pressed a soft kiss on his mouth. ''So, yes, Gabriel, I will marry you.''

Something broke apart inside him then. His heart lifted, and his spirit flew free, soaring up into the clear, star-filled night, and casting aside the heavy chains of regret to which it had been shackled for so long.

If he'd always known Marcia had been a mistake from the outset, he knew with even greater certainty that, this time, he'd made the right choice. Filled with a humility entirely foreign to him, he kissed Eve's eyes, her nose, her jaw, her mouth, with holy reverence.

"*La mia tesoro,*" he vowed, "I promise you on my most solemn word that you will never live to regret having said that. *Te amo,* my lovely Eve—not just now, in the heat of the moment, but tomorrow, and forever."

She thought he'd taught her everything there was to know about her body's capacity for passion, but she'd neglected to include love in the mix, and the difference was like that between water and champagne. Supper forgotten, they went upstairs to feast on the wonder of their newfound happiness. To talk in hushed tones of their hopes and dreams.

"How many children shall we have, *cara?*"

"How many would you like?"

"If they're all like you, then eight would be a good number. But if they're like me, we should be content with just one." He leaned over her, cast a lingering glance down her body, from her head to her toes. "You are beautiful...the most beautiful woman I've ever known."

It wasn't true, but she didn't care. If she was beautiful in his eyes, it was enough. She slid her hand over his hip, down his flank, then swept it across his lower belly. He was hard and pulsing; ready for her.

She lifted her hand and he watched her, his eyes a searing, molten-blue, as she touched herself, then drew her finger, damp with a woman's honey, over the length of his penis. It almost tipped him over the edge. With a strangled groan, he covered her, and buried himself deep.

Passion outrunning reason, desire more avid than sense, she met his thrusts, tilting her hips to possess all his mighty strength. Wrapping her legs around his waist and melding him to her so that she was forever stamped with his imprint. Again and again in the hot Mediterranean night, they made love, then lay entwined amid a tangle of sweat-drenched sheets, rendered mindless of anything but each other.

Always before, he'd used protection. But not that night. Nothing came between them, least of all a thin sheath of rubber designed by men of science to counteract nature's most basic instinct. That night, they flew with the gods.

The next morning, she sat propped against the pillows and fed Nicola her first bottle of the day, while he went downstairs to make coffee and dispose of last night's untouched meal. By the time Fiora showed up, grim-faced as ever, they were dressed and downstairs, and behaving respectably.

But it wasn't easy, and they escaped as soon as they decently could, to a quiet cove out of sight of the house. There, they lazed the day away, making plans, making love.

"Remember I talked about doing this?" he murmured against her mouth, locked tight inside her as he rode the sultry waves, while Nicola napped under the shade of a beach umbrella.

"I...remember..." Eve's answer fell away in a gasp as the now-familiar knot of tension wound tighter and tighter in her body, then snapped and left her bathed in a shower of sun-splashed stars.

"How soon will you marry me?" he wanted to know, when they lay sprawled on the sand, enjoying a picnic lunch of cheese and fruit and bread, washed down with homemade cider.

"How soon would you like?"

"Yesterday," he promptly said, and she laughed at the unsmiling solemnity of his reply.

"Will you settle for a month or two from now?"

"If that's your final offer. Where shall we hold the wedding? Would you like it to be Chicago?"

"No," she said. "I love Chicago, but it's not home."

"Where is, then? The place where you grew up?"

"Not anymore. My parents divorced during my last year of university. Now my mother lives in Denver, near my grandparents, and my father moved to North Carolina with his new wife."

"If you'd like it," Gabriel said carefully, "we could be married in Malta. I'd be happy to fly your family and friends over here—and before you slap me for trying to buy you off again, let me remind you that you're no longer just my daughter's aunt or Marcia's cousin. You're my future wife, and what's mine is yours."

"A wedding in Malta would be romantic," she said, picturing it in her mind's eye. The ceremony in an ancient stone church, with the bells ringing out over the city. Her in white satin and him in a gray morning suit, hands clasped, laughing and running through a shower of confetti to the limousine. A reception in the garden at the villa, surrounded by friends, family, flowers, all dappled by the ever-present sunlight— oh, yes! *Happy the bride the sun shines on!*

"Is all this really happening, Gabriel, or am I dreaming?"

"Oh, it's real, *cara mia,*" he said. "A dream come true."

And for the next three days, it was.

They arrived back in Valletta late Monday afternoon, in plenty of time to get ready for dinner with the Santoros. Beryl was waiting to meet them, full of her usual good humor.

"I've missed this little thing," she said, scooping Nicola into her arms. "And you, too, Eve. I don't relish the thought of how empty this place is going to be when you leave."

Although Eve was practically bursting at the seams with the news, she and Gabriel had agreed to hold off telling of their engagement until he'd bought a ring, and a formal announcement had appeared in the newspapers. So she made do with a smile and a cryptic, "It might not be quite as bad you think."

Beryl patted her cheek. "Well, love, you'd better promise to come back again, is all I can say."

"Consider it a promise kept," she said, sure her inner bliss was popping out of every pore and clearly visible to the naked eye.

But if so, Beryl didn't notice. "You leave all that to me, and get yourself ready for tonight," she ordered, shooing Eve aside as she was about to carry Nicola's things to the nursery. "Since you're not dining at home, I've got nothing better to do. Go on! You've got nearly two hours to make yourself beautiful. And not that it's any of my business, but if I were in your place, I'd consider wearing one of those dresses still stacked in boxes in the corner of your sitting room."

Well, why not? Eve thought, tempted less by the fact that being unofficially engaged to Gabriel made them somehow more acceptable, than she was by wanting to see his eyes light up and his gaze caress her in that special way that set her on fire all over.

She decided on a silky chiffon in varying shades of such a deep turquoise that it resembled the tumbling waves of the sea. Such a gown deserved to be teamed with diamonds or, at the very least, a string of good pearls, but since she didn't own either, she left it to speak for itself, and didn't even wear her rhinestone bracelet for fear it might snag the delicate fabric.

"My, but you look a picture!" Beryl exclaimed when Eve stopped by the nursery to say good night. "Fit to meet the queen!"

Gabriel, on the other hand, was struck speechless when she showed up in his study, where they'd arranged to meet. He swallowed a couple of times, adjusted his black bow tie as if it were choking him, and when he finally managed to speak, sounded as if he'd just gargled on ground glass.

"I…er, I have…something for you, *cara,*" he mumbled.

Mumbled? Gabriel Brabanti, who was never at a loss for words? "I have something for you, too," she said, biting back a smile and standing on tiptoe to plant a kiss on his mouth.

He blinked, and she thought how handsome he looked in his black dinner suit, with his shirt so crisply starched that it all but crackled. *This man is going to be my husband!* she told herself for the hundredth time, the reality of it still not really sinking in. *I am going to be known as Signora Gabriel Brabanti!*

Clearing his throat, he turned to the desk and snapped open a narrow leather case to reveal a diamond collar perhaps an inch wide, set in platinum. "While you were dressing, I had my jeweler send this over," he said, sounding a little more like his usual urbane self. "I consider it would go very well with what you're wearing, don't you?"

She stared at the necklace, too stunned to speak. It was the most beautiful thing she'd ever seen, and she didn't want to think what it must have cost him.

"Let me put it on you," he said, seeming to gather his wits in direct proportion to the speed at which she appeared to be losing hers. "I do believe it was made for a neck as slender and lovely as yours."

It nestled against her skin, cold and smooth. She'd have touched it, if she'd dared, but it would have been sacrilegious to leave fingerprints on so fine a piece. "How does it look?" she finally managed to say, turning for his inspection.

"Exactly as I knew it would," he said. "Absolutely perfect."

"Are you going to make a habit of spoiling me like this, Gabriel?" she asked, afraid she was going to cry and ruin her mascara.

"Not every day, perhaps, but certainly often enough to remind you how very much I value you as my wife." He reached toward the desk again, and she saw another, much smaller, square jeweler's box half-hidden among the papers lying there. "I know we said we'd wait a few days, but I'm not a patient man, *cara*," he continued, opening the box to reveal a diamond the size of a pea set in a broad platinum band. "Will you wear this tonight and let anyone who sees it recognize what it means, or would you rather choose something different—rubies or sapphires with diamonds, perhaps?''

She shook her head, again too overwhelmed to speak. When she'd first realized she was falling in love with him, she'd braced herself for disappointment and heartbreak, because aristocrats like Gabriel Brabanti didn't fall in love with ordinary little nurses from Chicago, not when they could take their pick from the *crème de la crème* of European society.

How could she have known the turn her life would take? How could she have prepared herself for the riches suddenly pouring into her lap, not just the worldly kind, but the deeply emotional wealth that came of being adored?

''I wouldn't change it for the world,'' she quavered.

''Then give me your hand and let's see if it fits.''

Unfortunately it turned out to be at least one size too big. Reluctantly he returned it to its velvet-lined box, and opened the safe hidden behind a section of bookcase.

''It would seem we must keep our secret a day or two longer, after all,'' he said, placing the box on top of the envelope containing her and Nicola's passports and plane tickets which she'd turned over to him for safekeeping, the night she arrived in Malta. "Come along, *la mia fidanzata bella.* If we're to be no more than fashionably late arriving at the Villa Santoro, we'd better get a move on."

"Just a second. I haven't yet thanked you properly for this." Her hand skimmed over the diamond collar. "Or for the ring. They're exquisite, and I'm bowled over by your generosity." She lifted her mouth to his, hoping her kiss told him how full her heart was, because no words could express it adequately. "Thank you, my love."

"*Prego, cara.* Giving you pleasure is all the thanks I need." He pulled her close for a second and third kiss, before releasing her with flattering regret, and guiding her out to the car.

After dinner, while the men sat out on the terrace and talked about whatever it was that men always found to talk about when their women weren't around, Carolyn took Eve on a tour of the house.

"It's really too large for us, now that our family's grown up and married," she said, leading the way up an elegant turn-of-the century staircase, "but we love it so, that it would be hard to see strangers living here. And since we're about to become first-time grandparents—our daughter, who lives with her husband in England, is due to give birth at any moment—it's quite likely that these empty bedrooms will soon be filled with the sound of children again.''

Following her into a room which, from the sporting trophies arranged on a shelf and the photographs mounted on the walls, must once have belonged to a boy, Eve said in all sincerity, ''You hardly look old enough to be a grand-mother.''

''Why, thank you, dear,'' Carolyn said, an odd smile playing around her mouth. ''And if you'll forgive me for saying so, you hardly look like the same young woman I met just a few weeks ago. Gabriel tells me he spirited you away to his country place on Gozo for a few days. Is that glow you're wearing the result of long hours in the sun and sea, or is there another reason you're so radiant that he can hardly keep his eyes off you?''

Eve couldn't hide the telltale blush staining her cheeks. ''Things have...changed,'' she ad-mitted. ''Between Gabriel and me, that is.''

Carolyn laughed outright and perched on the edge of the bed. ''I never would have guessed!'' she teased, patting the space beside her in in-vitation for Eve to sit also. ''And may I be the first to congratulate you. I know it's not the done thing, saying that to a woman, but in your case it's justified. I'd about given up hope that anyone could bring him out of his shell. He's been so reclusive since his marriage ended, and when he learned there was a baby on the way, it nearly killed him. He felt terribly responsible, on both counts, and seemed unable to accept that he wasn't entirely to blame.''

She reached out and folded Eve in an affectionate hug. ''You've given him back his life, Eve, and I thank God for it.''

Just then, one of the house staff appeared from downstairs to tell her she had an overseas phone call, and she sprang up, her face alive with a mixture of excitement and anxiety. ''That must be the baby news we've been waiting for!'' she said, her breath catching. ''Why else would someone be calling us at this hour? Will you excuse me, Eve? This shouldn't take long. Go back down to Gabriel, if you like. He's probably chafing at the bit anyway, at your being gone from his side for so long.''

He was doing no such thing. Was, in fact, in such deep conversation with Nico Santoro on the terrace that he didn't even notice her hovering on the threshold of the room behind.

"So your mind's made up, then?" Nico was asking him.

"*Si.*" He answered without a moment's hesitation. "I don't see what other choice I have."

"You'll be facing an uphill challenge, Gabriel. Trying to take a child away from her mother—especially during what the courts refer to as 'the tender years'—is never easy."

"In this case, my friend, the mother doesn't have a leg to stand on, and has only herself to thank for it."

"You'll still be a foreigner in a foreign land, fighting a foreign system."

"Not so. I intend waging this battle on my own turf. Nicola has dual citizenship and is living here—"

"Temporarily."

"Permanently, if I have any say in the matter. And given her complete lack of interest in our daughter, Marcia might not bother to contest my application." He leaned his elbow on the table between their two chairs. "And if she does," he said in a chilling voice, "I have enough people who'll attest to her callous indifference to Nicola's welfare—including her own cousin. Eve might not have liked me much when we first met, but she's solidly on my side now, and my trump card—although I'd prefer not to have to play it.''

Nico nodded. ''No question but that Eve's a fine woman by anyone's standards. That she happens not only to be a blood relative of the child, but also your future wife, is certain to carry a lot of weight with a judge.''

''*Si,* things couldn't have worked out better in that respect. She came on the scene at exactly the right time, and how fortunate for my daughter that she did. Eve is excellent mother material. Nicola will be better off by far in her care.''

''Nico, that was Steven on the phone!'' Carolyn's voice preceded her into the room by only a fraction of a second. Quicker than light, Eve moved out of sight behind the open door. Not that Carolyn would have noticed her anyway; all her attention was focused on reaching her husband and flinging her arms around his neck. ''Darling, we have a grandchild. Jane gave birth an hour ago, to a lovely healthy boy weighing seven pounds, eleven ounces!''

In the furore of excitement that followed, it was a simple matter for Eve to slip out of the room and pretend she'd been elsewhere in the house. To slump against the wall in the hall outside, as the truth of what was *really* going on between her and Gabriel ricocheted through her like a spurt of gravel hitting glass.

Pain clenched at her heart in an unforgiving fist. She felt cold all over. Dead. Except that she was still breathing. Still feeling. Still hurting.

All that passion, that tenderness, that so-called *love* was about taking Nicola away from Marcia, and using Eve to do it.

I don't know how Gabriel's going to cope when Nicola goes home…but he's a strong, resourceful man. I'm sure he'll find a way, Marjorie Ripley-Jones had said, that night at the opera. And how right she'd been! He'd coped better than anyone could have predicted.

Be careful…he's a shark…he'll eat you alive if you let him…do anything to get his own way….

"*Ahh!*" She clapped a hand to her mouth to stifle the cry that tore loose within her.

Marcia had tried to warn her. Why hadn't she listened? What sort of naive fool was she, to have bought for one minute the idea that Gabriel really loved her for herself, and not for what he thought she could give him?

"This calls for a toast. Ring for Roger and get him to bring us more champagne," she heard Carolyn say. "And where's Eve? I thought she'd joined the two of you."

"I'm right here," she said, forcibly dragging herself out of the abyss of grief into which she'd tumbled. And oh, how utterly calm she sounded! Amazing what the human spirit could do when it had to. Hers was rallying commendably. "What's all the fuss about?"

"Cara," Gabriel called out, hurrying to meet her, "you're just in time to help us celebrate. Carolyn and Nico have a grandson."

"That's wonderful!" She hoped the smile she pasted on her face looked a lot more genuine than it felt. "Congratulations!"

"From both of us," Gabriel said, slipping his arm around her shoulder and giving it a squeeze.

It was all she could do not to cringe from his touch. She'd have loved to slap his hand away; to fling her glass of champagne in his face and tell him what he could with his phony demonstrations of affection.

But to behave so badly in front of the Santoros, when they'd been nothing but kind to her, was unthinkable. So she kept her smile in place and when Nico went to refill their glasses, covered hers and said, "Thank you, but no! It was delightful to see you both again, and I thank you for a delicious dinner, but this is a family occasion and I think we should leave you to celebrate it alone."

Carolyn and Nico exchanged glances, the kind shared by a couple who loved and trusted one another completely. "Well," Nico said, "we do have a few phone calls we should make. If you're sure—?"

"We're sure," Eve said, then added much more sharply than she'd intended, "Come along, Gabriel!"

His raised eyebrows told her he'd noticed her tone and didn't much like it. Probably no one had spoken to him like that since he was a child—if then! But he was enough of a gentleman not to take issue with her in front of their hosts.

"We must meet again soon," he said, all suave Italian charm as he kissed Carolyn on both cheeks and shook Nico's hand. "We have a great deal to celebrate in both our families."

Much you know! Eve thought bitterly, sweeping ahead of him down the front steps to the forecourt.

"So, *cara,*" he began, the very second his car swept through the iron gates to the road, "did you have a good time tonight?"

"Lovely, thank you."

"You seem a little tired. A little out of sorts, almost."

"Do I?" Aware of his sideways glance, she turned her head and made a pretense of admiring the passing scenery. The Santoros lived on a very picturesque stretch of coast.

"Did you and Carolyn have a good visit upstairs?"

"Yes. She's a lovely woman."

He whistled tunelessly under his breath a moment. "What did you talk about while you were gone?"

"Nothing much," she said. "What did you and Nico talk about while we were gone?"

If he heard the irony in her voice, he chose to ignore it. "Business matters, mostly. I value his advice."

That about covered it, she supposed. Marrying her was nothing but a business arrangement—one that was about to blow up in his face!

"Have you thought anymore about setting a wedding date?"

"No," she said. "I wasn't aware there was any hurry."

"But you know, *tesoro,* that I am a most anxious bridegroom."

"Then you'll have to learn a little patience. Weddings can't be put together overnight. It'll take time to contact everyone in my family—my parents...*Marcia*.''

He didn't so much as blink at the mention of her name. He simply shrugged and dropped the subject. They didn't speak again until they arrived at the villa, and she thought she'd escaped further inquisition.

She should have known better. When she went to get out of the car, his hand shot across the console and closed around her wrist in an iron grip. ''*D'accordo, cara,* enough of this! You're not going anywhere until you tell me exactly what it is that has you looking as if you found a wasp in your underwear!''

CHAPTER ELEVEN

How about a viper in my bosom? she was tempted to reply. But the immediate urge to throw his ulterior motives back at him had cooled. Much as she hated evasion, she decided that speaking her mind in this instance wasn't necessarily the best thing. There was more at stake here than her wounded feelings. A baby's future hung in the balance, and Eve wasn't about to stand idly by and let Nicola become the pawn in what promised to be an ugly custodial tug of war.

"Eve?" His tone and his grip gentled. Releasing her wrist, he ran his hand up the back of her neck and toyed with her hair. "*Cara,* please talk to me."

"Not tonight," she begged, mortified by the leaping response of her blood. Her brain might know he was despicable, and her heart might feel so crushed she could hardly bear the pain, but her body still craved his touch.

His breath cruised over her cheek, teased her ear. "You're tired, and I'm an insensitive brute not to have realized it sooner. We slept hardly at all last night, were up early this morning, and here it is, almost tomorrow already. And so much has happened in between.''

She nodded miserably. *Yes, indeed, Gabriel! More than you can begin to know!*

He slid from behind the wheel and came around to open her door. ''Shall I carry you upstairs?''

''No!''

Her reply shot out with more emphasis than his question warranted. But for pity's sake, if she wound up in his arms, he'd almost certainly wind up in her bed, and where would her moral outrage end up then? Buried alive under an onslaught of indecent sexual craving, that's where! Besides, she had other plans for the night.

''O...kay.'' He spoke with the refined forbearing of a man confronted by a raging case of PMS. ''Just as you like, my love. May I walk you to your door?''

''Of course.'' She smiled with false enthusiasm. ''I'd be disappointed if you didn't.''

He made it easy for her to avoid him over the next two days. ''I've been called to London, to fill in as keynote speaker on water conservation at an international conference,'' he told her, stopping by the nursery early the following morning. "The man originally slated for the job came down with laryngitis at the last minute. I'm booked on a flight out of here at ten and won't be back until tomorrow night. I'm going to miss you like the devil, *cara*, and hate leaving you here alone."

"Don't worry about me," she said. "I won't be alone, and I've got plenty to do."

"Planning the wedding, *si?*" He leaned against the nursery door, and snagged her by the waist. "Shopping for a bridal gown, perhaps?"

"No," she said, resisting the tug of sexual longing pervading her senses. "There's no hurry on that."

"For me there is. If I had my way, we'd married today."

Not when he found out what she'd done, he wouldn't! He wouldn't be able to get rid of her fast enough, then.

"You still look tired, *cara*. Did you not sleep well?"

"No," she said, the tenderness in his voice making terrible inroads on her composure. How she kept herself together was nothing short of miraculous.

"Nor I." He nuzzled her neck. "I missed having you beside me."

She stiffened, and squeezed her eyes shut to hold back her tears. Even when she had every reason in the world to hate him, still she wanted him, and the thought that they'd never again make love left her blind with misery.

He released her. Held her at arm's length, his smile not quite as confident as usual, his eyes just the tiniest bit watchful. "We'll have a late dinner together tomorrow, yes? Spend the evening at home?"

She nodded and pressed her fingers to her mouth to control its trembling. The tears would have to wait. If she started crying now, she'd never stop.

He frowned. "Eve, everything *is* all right between us, isn't it?"

With a mighty effort, she gained control of herself. "Everything's exactly the same as it was last night, Gabriel," she told him, and wondered how she could have lived for twenty-seven years without realizing that truth could, when necessary, wield a lethal double edge.

He'd always prided himself on being able to keep his private and professional lives separate. But over the next two days he found his mind frequently wandering from the very tangible problem of water conservation world-wide, to the elusive sense that all was not well on the home front.

Although everything appeared the same on the surface, something had changed—a minor earthquake too slight to register on an emotional Richter scale. But the subtle shifting left everything a little bit off-kilter, and instinct warned him damage of some sort had occurred. In the end, it commanded his attention to such a degree that he opted out of the last afternoon's conference activities, and took an early flight back to Malta, arriving at the villa just after six.

"Where is everyone?" he asked, bumping into Beryl in the back hall, on his way from the garage.

"In the nursery, and if you're smart, you won't waste any time getting up there," she informed him darkly.

Before he could inquire what she meant by that, she disappeared into the kitchen and let the door shut slam shut behind her. But she'd said enough for his uneasy suspicions to crystallize into forbidding certainty. Dropping his briefcase and travel bag outside the study, he took the stairs three at a time.

Not bothering to knock, he let himself into Eve's suite. In passing through on his way to the nursery, it occurred to him that although nothing was out of place, her sitting room looked different.

"Eve?" His disquietude inching up another notch, he strode through to the nursery, needing to hold her in his arms and see for himself that everything was all right.

But she wasn't there waiting for him, and when he saw who was, he knew why the hair on the back of his neck had been standing up from the minute he set foot in his house. "What the hell are you doing here?" he barked.

"Oh, dear! Not pleased to see me, Gabriel?" Marcia asked, rocking placidly in the chair, with Nicola on her lap. "What a shame!"

"Answer the question, Marcia. Why are you here?"

"I've come to take Nicola home, of course."

His jaw must have dropped because before he could answer, she went on, "I don't know why that should come as such a shock, *caro*. You didn't really think I was going to let you steal my baby, did you?"

"I really didn't think you gave a damn," he said flatly. "I still don't."

"Then you greatly underestimate a mother's love." She smiled, and he wondered why he'd ever found her attractive. She was hard as nails and about as lacking in emotion as a brick. "I hear you're planning to sue for custody, Gabriel.''

''Who told you that?''

''I did,'' Eve said, and spinning around, he found her standing in the open door to her bathroom, her face paler than death.

Marcia's laughter rang out, brittle as glass splintering on stone. ''Congratulations, cuz! I've never known anyone able to take the wind out of his sails the way you just did!''

''Shut your mouth!'' he roared, and even as his world imploded around him, he found a tiny atom of pleasure in the way his ex-wife shrank back in the rocking chair. But it was short-lived and confronting Eve again, he asked the only question that mattered. ''Why?''

''Because you left me no choice.''

''No *choice? Dio,* Eve, I thought you loved me!''

''Then I guess we're both fools, because I thought you loved me.''

He threw up his hands, totally out of his depth. ''I don't know what I've done to make you doubt that.''

''Then let me explain.''

''Not here.'' He jerked his head at Marcia. ''Not in front of her. We discuss this in private.''

She shrugged and led the way to her sitting room. Following her, he realized suddenly why it looked different. She'd removed all her personal possessions, and two suitcases stood on the floor near the double doors.

"All right," he said, facing her across the coffee table. "Let's have it."

"I heard you telling Nico Santoro that you were going after custody."

His heart plummeted at that, but he took care not to show his dismay. "And you don't think I have just cause?"

"I don't care whether you have or not. Just because you've divorced Marcia doesn't mean I have. She's still my cousin. She always will be. And I'm not about to remain silent while you go behind her back and try to take her baby away from her."

"If you were this strongly opposed to my actions, why didn't you confront me at the time?"

"Because I know how persuasive you are, Gabriel." She tried to laugh, and ended up catching her lower lip between her teeth in an attempt to stifle a sob. "After all, look how you convinced me you loved me, how you wormed your way into my trust, when all you were really doing was using me."

"And just how do you arrive at that far-fetched conclusion?"

"I heard you bragging that with me now solidly on your side and testifying on your behalf, you'd be a shoo-in to win. And please don't insult my intelligence by telling me I misunderstood."

"I wouldn't dream of it."

Her pupils flared and she gave a little gasp. "You're not even going to *try* to deny it, are you?"

"I might be an utter blackguard by your standards, my dear, but I'm no liar. You've correctly interpreted seventy percent of what you overheard. As for the rest of your accusations—all that business about love and trust..." He snapped his fingers, a wild black fury overtaking him. "Why would I waste my time trying to change your mind on that, if this is your idea of loyalty to the man you're supposedly engaged to marry? I don't want or need a woman like that in my life. Once was enough!"

She almost flinched, but rallied at the last second. "What you need," she snapped, stalking to the desk to retrieve something from its drawer, "is a dog trained to do your every bidding without question. Put this around its neck when you find one. Or else save it for the next fool who falls for your phony Latin charm.

The diamond necklace flew through the air. "I wouldn't dream of it, Eve," he said, deftly catching it just before it crashed against the wall. "I don't believe in hand-me-downs. When I find a woman with whom I want to spend the rest of my life, she won't have to settle for anyone else's cast-offs. Although I have to say, after my experiences with you and your cousin, I'm anything but anxious to enter the matrimonial sweepstakes again. I don't seem to have much luck in choosing a winner."

"Or else," Marcia sneered from the doorway, "you get what you deserve."

"If that's true," he replied, not deigning to acknowledge her presence by affording her even a cursory glance, "I'll end up with permanent custody of Nicola. Because whatever else my shortcomings, I've proven myself to be a thousand times better parent than you'll ever be, and no judge in his right mind will award her to you."

"You don't have a snowball's chance in hell of taking her away from me, Gabriel."

The ring of certainty in her voice sent a chill up his spine, but he'd have walked through fire before he'd let her see it. "And why is that, Marcia?

"It's very simple," she said, the supreme satisfaction in her voice reminding him of a cat toying with a mouse whose life hung by a thread. "You're not her father."

Sometimes, the most outrageous statements carried with them an incontestable ring of truth. And this, he thought, fighting his way through the numbing haze of shock floating out to entrap him, was one of those times.

If she lived to be a hundred, Eve knew she'd never forget the seconds following Marcia's unconscionable remark. Each one was marked by the astounded thud of her heart. Every last, minute detail of the scene was burned in her memory. The blank disbelief on Gabriel's face, and the way he rocked slightly from side to side, as though trying to steady himself more firmly on a world suddenly tilting under his feet. The necklace that slipped from his hand and slid to the rug where it lay in a cold, glittering tangle of platinum and diamonds. Marcia's look of malicious triumph. The jarring, unbearable sound of her laughter mingling with Nicola's sudden frantic whimpering.

Aghast, Eve said, "For heaven's sake, Marcia, this is no time to be playing cruel jokes."

"Who's joking, cuz?" Marcia hooted, almost doubled over with unholy mirth.

"You are! You have to be!" She darted forward and plucked Nicola from her arms. "Hush, darling," she whispered, cuddling the baby. "It's okay. Mommy's just being silly."

"Mommy's telling the truth, kiddo! Jason's your real daddy, and he's downstairs, waiting to take us home."

"You've elevated the art of lying to new heights, Marcia." Gabriel's voice sounded as hollow as a tomb. "Either that, or you're insane!"

"And you're a fool, Gabriel, if you thought I'd make such an allegation without absolute proof that it's true." She withdrew an envelope out of the side pocket of the bag hanging from her shoulder. "Here, take a look for yourself. It's Nicola's birth certificate. Check out the date, *caro*. She was born May 14, nearly eleven months after you booted me out of Malta."

"Impossible!" he scoffed. "You informed me in the middle of April that I had a daughter who was almost three weeks old. How the hell could you do that, if she didn't arrive for another three weeks after that?''

''Ever heard of an ultrasound, Gabriel—those clever, informative little videos of infants still *in utero?* I'd known for a full two months prior to her birth that she was a girl.''

He turned to Eve, gray faced, and she could have wept at the agony she saw sketched on his features. ''It's sometimes possible, Gabriel,'' she confirmed, ''especially with today's sophisticated technology.''

He flinched as if he'd been dealt a blow to the side of the head that had left him brain dead. Only his eyes were alive, and they almost seared the flesh from her bones. ''You've been a part of this hellish charade, and have the brazen nerve to accuse *me* of using *you?*''

''I didn't know,'' she whispered. ''I swear to you that I had no idea what Marcia was up to.''

''You must have!'' he bellowed. ''You carried Nicola's passport.''

''But I never examined it closely. I had both hands full coping with Nicola while we were traveling. And once we'd arrived here, I had no reason to look at it again. You know yourself that I gave it to you along with mine and our airline tickets, sealed in a manila envelope which you locked away in your safe.''

"Don't yell at her," Marcia said.

"Sta zitto, strega!"

"Don't tell me to shut up! I don't take orders from you anymore."

"Under my roof, you do exactly as I tell you, or face the consequences," he thundered, covering the distance separating her from him in long, threatening strides. *"Dio,* but I should have killed you instead of divorcing you!"

"Lay a hand on me and I'll sue you for assault!" she yelled back, taking a swing at him with her bag.

Nicola, who'd calmed down and almost fallen asleep, burst into tears again at the noise and tension swirling about the room. "Stop it, both of you!" Eve hissed, doing her best to soothe the sobbing baby. "Neither of you is fit to be this child's parent. All you care about is scoring off one another, and it's making me sick to my stomach."

Marcia made a face and tossed her head. Gabriel, though, looked momentarily contrite, and turned back as if to try to comfort Nicola. But at the last minute, his hand hovered in the air and then slowly fell back at his side.

"I don't believe any of this," he muttered, staring around the room as if he'd never seen it before.

"I do," Eve said, all the pieces at last slotting neatly into place. "It explains everything, Gabriel, don't you see? Why Nicola seemed so small for her age. Why she was so weak and irritable. Why she never slept through the night." She swung an accusing glare on Marcia. "You sent me halfway around the world with a baby who was practically still a newborn. For God's sake, Marcia, what were you thinking?"

"That she'd be in excellent hands," Marcia said defiantly. "So she fussed a lot. Plenty of babies do, at that age. And if she was half as bad as you're trying to make out, you ought to be able to understand how impossible it would have been for us to take her on tour."

Again, Gabriel almost lunged at her in fury. Again, Eve intercepted him. "I understand *how* you did it, Marcia," she said coldly, "but I don't understand why."

Gabriel let out a blast of bitter laughter. "After everything you already knew about your cousin, plus what you've just learned, you can't put two and two together and come up with four? She did it for the money, Eve. She's the only woman I know who'd sell her child's birthright for the sake of a few thousand extra dollars in her bank account every month."

"Not just for the money," Marcia sneered. "It was payback time for a lot of things, not the least being the way you shipped me out of here as if I were nothing but a load of dirty laundry."

"An apt description, I'd say," he retorted, "and one you thoroughly deserved."

She shrugged. "Whatever! The point is, the money lasted long enough to finance my husband's new play which, I'm happy to tell you, has turned out to be quite a hit. It's opening on Broadway in the fall. I'd send you front row tickets to come and see it, Gabriel, if I thought you were at all interested."

Eve thought if he ever looked at her with the kind of loathsome disgust he turned on Marcia then, that she'd curl up and die. "Your capacity for cruelty astounds even me, Marcia," he said, "and someone needs to put a stop to it."

"Well, it's not going to be you, honey, because this time, I'm the one holding all the cards. How does it feel to know you're powerless, for a change?"

"Powerless? I don't think so. If you think this ends here, you're sadly mistaken."

Marcia came to Eve and very firmly took Nicola from her. "It ends, Gabriel, because this is my baby and I intend to walk out of here with her, and there's not a damned thing you can do to stop me.''

''You think not?'' he asked her scornfully. ''You seriously believe, do you, Marcia, that the fact that you gave birth to this beautiful infant protects you from the long arm of the law? Have you never heard of the sort of social system in America designed to protect innocent children from mothers like you?''

For the first time, Marcia actually looked afraid. ''Just because I let you borrow her for a few weeks doesn't mean I don't love her,'' she stammered, clutching Nicola tightly. ''It's been horrible without her. Every time I listened to your messages, it broke my heart. Why else do you think I never called you back? I couldn't have held it together long enough to say 'hello'''.

''She's probably telling the truth on that, Gabriel,'' Eve felt compelled to tell him. ''She burst into tears when she saw Nicola again. All she's done since she got here this morning is cuddle her and talk to her, and promise she'll never leave her again. In her own warped way, she really does love her baby.''

''And her love is exceeded only by a thirst for revenge that borders on criminal!''

"I'm not excusing what she did. I'm just trying to make it easier for you to let Nicola go. She has two parents, Gabriel, and they flew here at a moment's notice when they thought they were in danger of losing her. You can't contest that. And you have to admit, at no time was Nicola in any kind of danger here. She was with people who loved her unconditionally. Everyone who met her, adored her."

He stared at Eve—no, *through* her, for perhaps a minute, the muscle in his jaw knotting furiously. At last, he said, "Get out of my sight and out of my house, both of you.

"As soon as you hand over the passports," Marcia spat.

"Gladly," he shot back. "I can't be rid of you soon enough. And may God help that poor child."

"Come on, Eve," Marcia muttered, almost sprinting to the door before he could change his mind. "Let's tell Jason we're ready to go. Leave the suitcases. One of the hired hands can lug them downstairs. It's what they get paid to do, after all."

Eve picked up her carry-on bag and purse, a lump the size of an orange clogging her throat. Before leaving the room, she turned for one last look at the man who'd taught her everything about love. He was watching Nicola, an expression of poignant sorrow marking his face.

No, Eve would never forget what her cousin had done. And she'd never forgive her for it, either.

CHAPTER TWELVE

By the end of October, summer was a distant memory in Chicago, and the wind howling in from the lake carried with it the bite of winter. But it couldn't sever the ties that bound Eve to Gabriel. Though gossamer fine, they were stronger than tempered steel. And just how indestructible they'd always be was borne out, the morning she paid a visit to her doctor.

"Yup, you're two and a half months pregnant," Daphne O'Neil confirmed. "And I don't suppose I'm telling you anything you haven't already figured out for yourself."

"No," Eve said. Pretending not to notice she'd missed two periods had been one thing; the fact that she was throwing up around the clock was rather more difficult to ignore.

Still, she hadn't dared dream too much. Instead, she'd let the possibility that she'd conceived tiptoe quietly at the back of her mind, and hadn't even taken a home pregnancy test because of the superstitious belief that forcing the issue might jinx it.

''So is this happy news,'' Daphne asked, ''or should we be talking about options?''

It was the best news in the world! She might have managed to keep busy enough during the days, but at night, with nothing to shield her from the memories, she was haunted by the grief in Gabriel's eyes during those last wretched moments they'd spent together.

If some of the things he'd done were regrettable, she'd made mistakes, too. She'd taken sides and, only when it was too late, realized she'd taken the wrong side. The person she should have suspected was not the man who'd never once given her reason to doubt him, but the cousin whose self-interest formed a legacy of deceit that went back a lifetime.

At the end of it all, the one constant was that she loved him regardless. If he could forgive her, she could forgive him. Because such a deep, enduring love wasn't something to be tossed aside. It was too rare; too precious. It was worth fighting for.

So often, she'd almost phoned to tell him this, and once, when she was talking to her mother, a long-distance call-alert signal had interrupted their conversation. Whoever it was at the other end hung up before she could connect to it, but deep in her heart she'd been sure it was Gabriel.

She'd known for a fact it wouldn't have been Marcia. Relations between her and Eve were strained past breaking point.

In the end, Eve had let matters lie because she hadn't known how to heal the gaping wound he'd suffered when he'd lost Nicola. Hadn't known what she could offer him that might possibly make up for the pain Marcia had caused him.

Until now.

Now, she could give him a child. *His* child, and if it took medical proof to convince him he was the father, she could give him that, too.

Within the week, she was en route to Malta, via London, and was delighted when, on the last leg of her journey, she found herself boarding the same flight as Carolyn Santoro, who'd just spent a week in England visiting her new grandson.

''I'm so happy to see you!'' she exclaimed, returning Carolyn's hug.

''I'm even happier to see you,'' Carolyn said, her initial burst of enthusiasm dwindling into a gravity that made Eve's blood run cold. ''Please tell me you're coming back to help Gabriel.''

''Help him?'' she repeated, hollow with sudden dread. ''Why? What's wrong with him?''

"Oh, my dear, where to begin?" Carolyn exhaled a long sigh of distress. "I told you once before that when his marriage broke up, he shut himself off from everyone who cares about him. But that was nothing compared to how he is now."

"Which is *how?*" The ever-present nausea rose up in protest and she broke out in a fine dew of perspiration. "Carolyn, please just tell me what's happened, before you give me a heart attack!"

"Well, for a start, no one ever sees him anymore. He's closed up the villa, with only a skeleton staff to keep an eye on the place, and is staying at the farmhouse on Gozo. He comes into Valletta when he has to, of course, for business purposes, or to stock up on anything he can't get locally, but he's dropped out of the social scene completely. Nico happened to run into him last week, and said he looks just dreadful. Very drawn, he said, and just not himself, at all."

"When did all this start?"

"Pretty much the day you and Nicola returned to the U.S." She cleared her throat uncomfortably. "I really despise gossip, Eve, but servants talk and it's common knowledge among his circle of friends that Marcia came

back and caused a terrible scene, so please forgive me if this question offends you, but I simply have to ask. Is it true that he's not Nicola's
father?''

''I'm afraid it is. I had no idea, Carolyn—
none at all. I found out the same time that he
did.''

''You don't have to tell me that. I know
you'd never be party to such an appalling deception.'' She clasped Eve's hands. ''Oh, you
have no idea how glad I am to see you!''

''And I, you! At least now I know what to
expect.''

Hearing from someone else, though, and seeing
for herself, were two different things. Nothing
could have prepared Eve for her first glimpse of
Gabriel.

She had the taxi drop her off at the end of the
road leading to the farmhouse, and went the rest
of the way on foot, arriving just as the shadows
deepened toward dusk. Unaware of her approach, he sat in the garden, staring out to sea,
an open book lying face down on his lap, and
the fat tabby cat snoozing at his feet.

Eve's heart clenched at the sight of him. He'd
lost weight and looked so solitary, so terribly
alone. *We did this to him,* she thought. *Between*

us, Marcia and I drained all the joy from his life and left behind a shell of a man.

Suddenly she wasn't at all sure he'd be glad to see her. Wasn't certain anything she could say or do could close the yawning distance between them.

She must have made a sound—stepped on a dried twig, perhaps, or a loose flagstone—because without shifting his gaze he said, "Is that you, Beryl?"

"No," Eve said, and swept up in a tide of emotion by the sound of his voice, she dropped her suitcase and ran toward him. "It's me, Gabriel."

He turned his beautiful, empty eyes on her. "*Eve?* How did you get here?"

"The usual way," she said, caught in a vicious undertow of regret at having waited so long to come back. "By jet, from Chicago, via London."

He nodded, still so far removed in spirit that she wasn't sure he'd even heard her. Unable to bear the strained silence, she glanced at the lighted interior of the farmhouse. "Did I hear you correctly, a minute ago? Beryl's here?"

"*Si.*"

"What happened to Fiora?"

"She died. So much did, with the end of summer." He sighed heavily. "Why are you here?"

"I've come to tell you I'm sorry for my part in Marcia's unspeakably cruel hoax, and to ask you to forgive me."

He might have been cast in stone, for all the reaction he showed. Only the cat moved, slinking away under the grape arbor as if it felt the electricity in the atmosphere and wanted to take cover before the storm broke. "Is that all?"

"Not by a long shot," she said, aching to touch him but afraid he'd recoil from any contact. "I've missed you, Gabriel. So much that there've been times I've had to wrap my arms around myself and hold on tight because I was afraid I was going to fly apart at the seams without you."

He didn't answer, and the silence beat between them like the widespread wings of a hovering eagle.

"I took a leap of faith in coming here," she went on desperately, "because I believe in you, in *us*."

His glance flickered. "I'm not sure I believe in anything in anymore."

"Don't say that!" she cried. "What happened to the man I used to know—the one who never gave up?"

"He's changed. A little girl stole a piece of his heart, and he'll never be the same again."

"Neither of us will be. Hurt like that never really goes away. But one thing I've learned is that the human heart has a boundless capacity for love, and although Nicola owns a piece of mine, too, there's still so much room in it for you."

"Really? The last time we spoke, you didn't believe I loved you. You thought I was merely going through the motions in order to win your support before a judge."

"I'll believe you now, if you tell me I was mistaken."

He mulled over the proposition for so long that she wished she'd never suggested it. Finally he hauled himself out of the chair and turned to face her. "You want the truth?"

"Always," she said, even though a quiver of apprehension shivered over her. "Truth is the one thing that never lets us down."

"Then I admit, in the beginning, I did make a conscious effort to win you over. I knew Marcia too well, and nothing about her past behavior convinced me that motherhood would change her for the better. But I wanted to be fair and give her the chance to prove me wrong. So

I offered her the choice of coming here, or having me go there. She chose the former."

"But sent me in her place."

"Yes. Right then I knew she was cooking up something devious."

"You didn't trust me."

He inclined his head. "I saw you as her accomplice, someone whose chief aim was to deflect my attention from the bizarre behavior of a woman who claimed to be devoted to her baby."

"I was disturbed by that, too, Gabriel."

"But you never admitted it to me. When I questioned her actions, you defended her. This fed my suspicions and led me to believe you knew more than you were telling me. So I decided I had to make you my ally. I was prepared to seduce you, if that was what it took. I just hadn't expected it would..." He raised his hand, palm up, searching for the right words.

"Be so easy?" she supplied, recoiling.

For a split second, he remained motionless, his eyes blank with shock. Then, as though galvanized to action by the absurdity of her assumption, he reached out and grasped her by the shoulders. "Don't even *think* such a thing!" he ordered, with something approaching his old air of authority. "What I'm trying to say is that I hadn't expected it would backfire. Falling in love with the enemy wasn't part of my plan. I knew better than that, and only a fool makes the same mistake twice. You were, after all, Marcia's cousin, and blood is thicker than water.''

''But I was never your enemy, Gabriel, and if, in the beginning, my loyalty lay with her, I knew in the end that she'd used me in ways you couldn't begin to devise. That she had a talent for cruelty beyond anything you could comprehend.''

''I'd realized, long before that, that you were nothing like her. Every day, I discovered in you attributes she'd never possessed—the kind a man looks for in a wife. I saw your tenderness and compassion with Nicola; your patience and diligence. I saw the way you related to Beryl, treating her not as a servant, there to do your every bidding, but as a friend. And I wished I didn't have to involve you in what I knew was bound to be a dirty fight. But, Eve, my first duty had to be to that defenseless child, and in that respect you were right to think I'd have used you to sway a judge in my favor. I'd have used the pope himself, if I could have.''

"I know," she said. "No one seeing you with Nicola could ever have questioned your devotion to her."

"It was more than that, Eve. All other considerations apart, Nicola would have been so much better off with you as her mother. But I swear to you, she was not the reason I asked you to marry me. Win or lose the court battle, I'd still have loved you and wanted you for my wife."

Loved, he said. And *wanted.* "And is that all in the past tense now?" she asked him. "Is there no future for us?"

The haggard look closed in on him again "In all truth, I haven't dared look into the future," he said, stepping back. "It haunts me to think of what it holds for that little girl, with parents such as she has."

"Then I'm glad I'm here, even if the only benefit is to put your mind at rest."

He swiped a weary hand down his face. "I would give a king's ransom to find some peace. To be able to close my eyes at night and not be chased by demons."

"I believe I can give you that peace."

"How?" He nodded at her suitcase leaning drunkenly near the gate. "You have a bag of magic tricks in there?"

"Not exactly, but the next best thing, perhaps. I did some investigating of my own after I left here at the end of August, and learned that Jason is an only child whose parents live on Staten Island, a stone's throw from Manhattan. I made it my business to let them know everything their son and daughter-in-law had been up to."

He almost smiled. "Marcia must have been thrilled!"

"Marcia swears she'll never speak to me again, which I consider to be a small price to pay for setting the record straight.

"And the grandparents?"

"Were genuinely horrified. They worship Nicola, and assured me they'll be keeping a very close eye on her in future. I really believe, if they suspect any more shenanigans, they'll step in and do exactly what you were prepared to do: apply to the courts for guardianship of a minor. There'll be no more palming Nicola off to me or anyone else, the next time Marcia decides career comes before motherhood. And the best of it is, they're young, Gabriel, in their late forties only. God willing, they'll be around for a lot of years yet, and although they don't have much in the way of money, they have a world of love to give their granddaughter."

It was as if a weight lifted from his shoulders, then. He let out a great sigh of relief, and right before her eyes, his old energy reasserted itself. His face came alive, the grooves curving each side of his mouth disappeared, and even his skin seemed to glow with renewed vigor.

"Money will never be an issue," he said, putting his arms around Eve and holding her tight. "Providing Nicola with the emotional support she deserves might have been denied me, but I've established a trust fund to look after her every financial need. If her grandparents can give her unlimited love and protection, she will be very well taken care of on every front."

"And us?" She leaned back to look at him, still not sure where that left the two of them. "You might as well know I don't have a return ticket to the States. One way or another, I'm going to be a part of your life forever. It's up to you to decide how you'd like to arrange that."

"Name your price," he said, his mouth hovering so close to hers that she could taste the kiss waiting in the wings. "You are my heart, *tesoro*. Without you I am nothing."

Was that her breath echoing raggedly in that quiet, twilit garden? "I want you to trust me," she whispered, aching to hear him say the words for no other reason but that he loved her. "I want you to believe in us."

"I already do." He brought his lips to hers, and it was like a sudden explosion of rain in the desert. All the parts of her that had withered since she'd left him bloomed again, full and rich and bursting with new passion. "You are my heart," he told her. "Without you, I am nothing. From this day forward, it's you and I, and no one else in the mix."

She drew back, the gift she carried deep inside begging to be revealed. "I'm afraid not," she said. "It can never again be just the two of us."

He stared at her, doubt clouding the clear blue of his eyes. "After all this, you're telling me we're finished before we've properly begun?"

"No, Gabriel, never that," she said, and taking his hand, placed it low against her womb. "I can't give Nicola back to you, my love, but I can give you another child, the one I carry here. *Your* child, Gabriel, conceived in love and honesty."

"A baby?" His smile lit up the dark, making all the empty, dreary days worthwhile; all the long, lonely nights worth every second of grief they'd caused her. *"Ours?"*

"Definitely. Check with my doctor, if you don't believe me. She predicts I'll give birth around May 28. And she expects a healthy, full-term baby."

"I don't need a doctor's report. Your word is good enough for me."

She relaxed against him, the last of her fears swallowed up by the rising moon. "Are you up to dealing with more sleepless nights?"

The smile which had captivated her nearly four months earlier illuminated his beloved features again. "I've had plenty of practice being a father," he said, lifting her clear off her feet and swinging her around exuberantly. "I come with my own set of built-in know-how."

"Signor Brabanti?" Beryl's voice floated across the garden from the open door of the farmhouse. "I'm preparing the evening meal. Will your guest be staying?"

"She's no guest, Beryl," he replied, holding Eve close. "My fiancée and your favorite American lady has come home again. Make dinner for three, and bring out the champagne. We're all going to celebrate."

Beryl shaded her eyes and peered through the gloom. *"Eve?"* There were tears in her voice. "Thank God you're home again, at last! Now we can all start living again. Come here and let me look at you.''

''Not so fast,'' Gabriel muttered, drawing Eve back into his arms and stealing her heart all over again with a kiss which promised her forever. ''If it's true that everyone has a guardian angel sitting on his shoulder, my darling, you are surely mine. I love you with all my heart and soul.''

It was everything, and more, than she'd dared to hope for. With those few heartfelt words, he'd given her the world.

MILLS & BOON® PUBLISH EIGHT LARGE PRINT TITLES A MONTH. THESE ARE THE EIGHT TITLES FOR DECEMBER 2004

MISTRESS OF CONVENIENCE
Penny Jordan

THE PASSIONATE HUSBAND
Helen Brooks

HIS BID FOR A BRIDE
Carole Mortimer

THE BRABANTI BABY
Catherine Spencer

GINO'S ARRANGED BRIDE
Lucy Gordon

A PRETEND ENGAGEMENT
Jessica Steele

HER SPANISH BOSS
Barbara McMahon

A CONVENIENT GROOM
Darcy Maguire

MILLS & BOON®

Live the emotion

1104 Rom

MILLS & BOON® PUBLISH EIGHT LARGE PRINT TITLES A MONTH. THESE ARE THE EIGHT TITLES FOR JANUARY 2005

❧

THE MAGNATE'S MISTRESS
Miranda Lee

THE ITALIAN'S VIRGIN PRINCESS
Jane Porter

A PASSIONATE REVENGE
Sara Wood

THE GREEK'S BLACKMAILED WIFE
Sarah Morgan

HIS HEIRESS WIFE
Margaret Way

THE HUSBAND SWEEPSTAKE
Leigh Michaels

HER SECRET, HIS SON
Barbara Hannay

MARRIAGE MAKE-OVER
Ally Blake

MILLS & BOON®

Live the emotion

1204 Rom LP